"All right, then I'll make you a deal."

Adam caught her gaze and held it. "I promise I won't ask you to give up your career, to live with me, or marry me, if you'll have dinner with me."

They were sitting in a small, cozy bar, and Kate was wondering how he'd managed to get her there. "I have a feeling I'm about to fall into a trap. But if I agree, what about next time?"

"Next time will take care of itself."

"That's what I was afraid of. No deal."

He gave her a thoughtful look. "All right," he said at last. "I won't ask you to give up your job, live with me, or marry me for the next three months. All that for just one dinner. You drive a hard bargain."

But it wasn't just for one dinner, and they both knew it.

KAREN VAN DER ZEE is an author on the move. Her husband's work as an agricultural advisor to developing countries has taken them to many exotic locations. The couple said their marriage vows in Kenya, celebrated the birth of their first daughter in Ghana and their second in the United States, where they make their permanent home. The whole family spent two fascinating years in Indonesia. Karen has had several short stories published in her native Holland, and her modern romance novels with their strong characters and colorful backgrounds are enjoyed around the world.

Books by Karen van der Zee

HARLEQUIN PRESENTS

HARLEQUIN ROMANCE

Don't miss any of our special offers. Write to us at the following address for information on our newest releases.

Harlequin Reader Service
901 Fuhrmann Blvd., P.O. Box 1397, Buffalo, NY 14240
Canadian address: P.O. Box 603,
Fort Erie, Ont. L2A 5X3

KAREN VAN DER ZEE

fancy free

Harlequin Books

TORONTO • NEW YORK • LONDON
AMSTERDAM • PARIS • SYDNEY • HAMBURG
STOCKHOLM • ATHENS • TOKYO • MILAN

Harlequin Presents first edition May 1987
ISBN 0-373-10982-2

Original hardcover edition published in 1986
by Mills & Boon Limited

CHAPTER ONE

THE man boarded the plane minutes after Kate had settled herself in her seat, book open on her lap. Her heart gave a small, nervous leap at the sight of him. She had expected him, of course, yet she'd hoped, somehow, he would not show up. He was tall and dark, wearing an impeccable lightweight suit, moving with the easy grace of a man comfortable with himself. His tightly curled hair was cropped close to his head, emphasising the strong, square lines of his darkly tanned face. She felt a quiver of apprehension.

An hour earlier she'd stood in line at the check-in counter, having the sudden eerie feeling of being watched. She'd never had that kind of feeling, at least not anything quite so strong. Handing her ticket and passport to the agent, she tried to ignore it. Still, she couldn't resist glancing around. The man was in line a few places behind her, his eyes directed at her in intense regard. For a moment their eyes had locked, then she'd looked away, feeling distinctly uncomfortable. It wasn't unusual that a man should look at her. Her bright red hair screamed for attention, even more so in a place like Singapore where her height of five-foot-seven made her stick out above the dark-haired masses. But the man's regard had been more than casual admiration or interest, and she had no idea why. The few minutes that it took to have her passport and ticket checked, her luggage weighed and dispatched, had seemed endless. She'd been acutely aware of his eyes practically boring holes into her back.

He was one of the most handsome men she'd ever seen (even more handsome than the Texas Twins she'd been fighting off the past few weeks), and her instinctive defence mechanisms sprang immediately into action. She didn't trust handsome men. Experience had taught her that more often than not they were unbearably arrogant and altogether too sure of themselves. This was, of course, a rather broad generalisation, and a few exceptions could probably be found somewhere on this planet. Kate, in a reasonable mood, would admit to that. Perhaps this very man was one of them. Maybe he was kind, loving, unselfish and altogether wonderful—you could never tell.

Fat chance, she said to herself. Loving, unselfish men did not look at a woman the way he had looked at her. Kate preferred her men a bit flawed—a crooked nose, unruly hair—men who survived in the world because of their capabilities and personality rather than their looks.

The man stopped next to her chair. Steady brown eyes focused on her face. He stood still for a fraction of a moment, then tossed his leather briefcase into the window seat next to hers.

This was no mere coincidence, Kate was quite sure. No doubt he'd charmed the girl behind the counter into giving him the seat next to hers. The audacity!

He reached for the storage compartment above her head. 'Pardon me.' His voice was deep and resonant, his accent American. He stretched easily, opening the bin and stuffing in a trench coat. The corner of his jacket brushed her shoulder and her eyes were level with the leather belt that encircled his waist. His shirt had a tiny grey and white stripe. A whiff of clean, male scent filled her nostrils. The warmth of his body was faintly discernible on her cheek. His physical nearness made her uncomfortable and she closed her eyes, pretending sleep.

'Pardon me,' he said again, sliding past her to get to the window seat. His legs briefly brushed against hers.

She gave no reply, tucked the small pillow on to her shoulder and turned her head.

He was making himself comfortable in his seat. She heard the slight movements of his body as he pushed the briefcase under the seat in front. There was the click of the safety belt, the rustling of a magazine.

'A drink, sir?'

Kate opened her eyes a fraction. A flight attendant hovered in the aisle, her voice an attractive sing-song, her slim body encased in the well-fitting batik uniform. She was a Malay girl with glossy black hair and gorgeous brown eyes.

'Scotch on the rocks, please.'

'Yes, sir.' She returned a moment later with the requested drink.

Kate kept her eyes closed, aware of the man's movements, the tinkling of the ice in the glass. Could she keep this up all the way to Amsterdam? Probably not. Eighteen hours of this and they'd have to open her lids surgically. Idly she wondered about the proficiency of Dutch hospitals. She'd sampled hospitals the world over—a broken arm in the Ivory Coast, an appendectomy in Malaysia, eight stitches in her calf in Thailand. Her father worked for the State Department and they'd always lived abroad. Her parents were now in Tunisia, living in a large white villa in Tunis. A hand touched her shoulder. 'Ma'am? We're taking off.' It was the same sing-song voice. 'Please put your seat in the upright position.'

Damn! Kate straightened, pushed the button on the chair arm and the back moved forward. She reached for her paperback and began to read. It was incredible how difficult it was not to look sideways. It was giving her a cramp in her neck. The book was disappointing, offering a lot more on the cover than it delivered inside. She should have bought the new Ken Follet.

He was looking at her again. She could feel it, like a touch, a brush against her cheek, her hair. Anger grew inside her until she could no longer contain it. She turned her face abruptly, meeting the dark eyes.

'Can't you find something else to stare at?' she asked coldly.

He was unabashed. The corner of his mouth tilted in a smile. 'Nothing nearly as appealing to the eye.'

'Try!'

'You have the most beautiful red hair I've ever seen.'

'I don't like being stared at.'

'It's surely not the first time,' he said mildly.

'That doesn't make it any easier to take.' She sounded like a first-class bitch. It wasn't her nature to be so catty, but she was tired and irritable and after the experience with the Texas Twins she was fed up with everything male. The man next to her was getting on her nerves. She didn't like that little smile of his, that gleam in his eye. She was less than thrilled at the idea of having to sit next to him for the next eighteen hours.

'I've always been a sucker for red hair.'

'Try living in Ireland.'

He nodded agreeably. 'Excellent idea, unfortunately not feasible.' He observed her for a moment. 'I'm sorry if I offended you. It certainly was not intended.'

'I'm pleased to hear that,' she said coolly.

'You're very beautiful.'

'So are you,' she retorted.

He laughed out loud. He had a mouthful of strong, white teeth. 'You don't seem impressed.'

'Handsome men are not to be trusted. Nothing

re but a lot of arrogance and a lot of inflated ego.'
she couldn't believe she was saying these things.

'Ouch,' he said, but his eyes were laughing. 'And
the same thing could not be said of women, of course.
They always suffer because of their beauty. I've often
heard them complain that their gorgeous exteriors
make men look no further to discover the treasures
beneath the surface. Do you hide any treasures? Or are
you just what you appear? Bitchy, suspicious and
rude?'

It took her aback for a moment. 'You call me rude?
What do you think it is to stare at a woman as if she
were a piece of meat?'

He grinned. 'You do have a sense of the dramatic.'

His laughter incensed her, the more so because she
had to admit he was right. She'd exaggerated.
Exaggeration, if she were to believe her friends, was
one of her talents. His eyes had held admiration, not
lascivious hungering. With his looks he probably
didn't have to do a lot of hungering for women.

The flight attendant enquired if they wanted
another drink. The meal would be served in half an
hour, she informed them. Could she take their orders?
There was a choice of veal, chicken or fish. The menu
card looked like something from an exclusive
restaurant. Unfortunately, the reality was often
disappointing.

Kate chose the chicken and asked for some white
wine. It might help her relax. She had no idea why she
was so uptight. There'd be a movie later, after the
plane had made a stop in Bombay. Unfortunately,
she'd seen it before and it wasn't much good, but she
hoped Mr Handsome next to her would want to watch
it. It would keep his eyes occupied and his mouth
shut.

He was watching her curiously. 'You must have had

some very negative experiences with handsome men⹁ t
sound so derogatory,' he commented.

'You've got it.' She wasn't going to discuss her love
life, or lack thereof, with him. She stared at her book.
In the course of her job, she came across many
handsome, wealthy men. There had been Max, the
actor, selfish, demanding, wanting the world to kneel
at his feet. Not being the kneeling type, she'd got rid
of him fast. And Elliot, the lawyer, charming, very
talented and equally self-centred. He'd wanted her to
give up her career, get a desk job or do nothing at all.
He invited her to move in with him in his elegant
penthouse apartment overlooking Central Park and
take care of his every need. He was used to having
women at his beck and call. After a nasty scene, she'd
sent him off, too. There'd been a few other men, but
no one serious. Most men got fed up with her
schedule. Most men she found boring. She wanted
somebody different. Somebody fun and free, who
made no demands on her, who didn't expect her to
give up her job to pamper him. She was twenty-seven
and not ready to settle down to play the domestic
scene. Maybe one day she would get tired of the
travel, the constant changes, the sleeping in different
beds almost every night. But not yet. Not for a while.

'I wonder,' the man next to her said slowly, 'if it
would be possible for us to have a normal, civilised
conversation.' He gave her an enquiring look, one
eyebrow slightly raised.

'Why?'

'For one thing, it makes flying so much more
pleasant. We have seventeen hours to go—that is if
you're going to Amsterdam, too. Secondly, it is easier
on the nerves.'

'Yours or mine?'

'Yours, mostly. Does flying make you nervous?'

She gave a dry laugh. 'Hardly.'

'I didn't think so. So what is the problem? Apart from my presence in the seat next to you, that is.'

There was a moment of silence as she considered an answer. He was looking at her expectantly. He had a perfect nose, a well-shaped mouth. He probably had a beautiful wife tucked away in the suburbs somewhere. She straightened in her seat. 'All right, let me tell you. I have no problems that can't be cured with some sleep. I'm a tad frazzled, you see. I've just come back from Inner Mongolia where I spent three weeks riding around on horses and camels and drinking enough tea with mare's milk to last me for the rest of my life. All I want is some peace.'

His face gave nothing away. 'Fascinating place, Mongolia. Did you see the Wu Ta Five Pagodas in Hohhot?'

His reply took her by surprise and he laughed when she didn't immediately have an answer ready. 'You expected me not to believe you, right?'

She shrugged non-committally, unbuckling her belt. 'Excuse me.' She picked up her bag and came to her feet. In the lavatory she let out a deep breath. Good Lord, what was going on here? What a ridiculous conversation to have with a stranger. All those vibes coming and going. It was unusual that a man, a total stranger at that, should elicit so much hostility in her for such trivial reasons. He'd been looking at her, like other men sometimes looked at her. Normally she wouldn't react nearly so cattily. She might give the man a half-amused, half-mocking smile and say something like, 'Do I have mud on my face?' And the man would laugh and say no, he was just admiring the beautiful colour of her hair. 'I'm glad you like it,' she'd answer. 'It wasn't easy to come by, you know. I have the dye mixed up specially in Paris.' Or something equally ridiculous. From there on they'd have an amiable conversation, passing the long, boring hours of one more endless plane trip. He'd tell her all about his brilliant career in plastics, politics or podiatry. She'd tell him all about her speciality travel agency, serving the adventurous wealthy; how she and three friends had started it after they had left college, with the financial backing of helpful, if doubtful, parents; how it had begun as a joke, a crazy idea that kept growing in their minds and had taken on a life of its own. She'd be grateful to have someone half-way interesting sitting next to her, rather than a brassy high-society madam in furs or a drunk who snored. And before the plane landed there was always the inevitable invitation for dinner, dance and delights, which usually she'd decline *in toto* or partially. They'd exchange business cards, promise to call, and say goodbye cheerfully.

The man sitting next to her now was probably no different than the rest, trying to pick her up, hoping for a night on the town in Amsterdam. Men like him picked women up in every plane and hotel, conveniently departing the next day. My, my, she said to herself, aren't you the cynic. You sound like Roxanne.

Kate sighed and stared at her face in the mirror. Fatigue was visible in the tight line of her mouth. Her eyes looked rather dull, not their usual bright blue. He'd called her beautiful. She wasn't, actually. She knew that. Roxanne said she had an interesting face, whatever that meant. 'You've got great eyes, you know, sort of innocent-looking, and then that sexy, full mouth to go with it for contrast,' she'd enumerated. 'And that gorgeous mop of curly red hair to top it all off, so to speak. No wonder the men go wild over you.' This, of course, was rather an exaggeration. She didn't have to chase them away with stick, but she did get her share of male attention. And she was getting some right now on this plane. She grimaced in the mirror. It couldn't have come at a worse time.

She brushed out the heavy tangle of curls and put on some lipstick. She straightened the green cotton jersey dress, smoothing it over her hips, and adjusted the belt. There was nothing else to do. She'd better get back there and try to be civil. She couldn't very well hang out in the lavatory for the next seventeen hours or so. A few moments later she came down the aisle, avoiding the stranger's eyes as they followed her progress with undisguised appraisal.

The wine had arrived and had been placed on her table. The man picked up the glass to make it easier for her to sit down, then handed it back.

'Thank you,' she said politely.

He looked at her levelly. 'My name is Adam Cooper. I'm from New York.'

'Kate. Kate Flannigan.'

'From?'

She'd been afraid he'd ask. 'New York.'

There was a spark of triumph in his eyes. 'City, I take it?'

'Officially, but I'm hardly ever there. I travel most of the time.' She picked up her book, not wanting to encourage further discussion. He did the same, much to her relief, and for some time they both read without speaking. Around her ebbed and flowed the soft babble of voices of the other passengers and the monotonous drone of the aeroplane engines. Sometimes it seemed she spent half her life on aeroplanes, hours spent among strangers whose only common denominator was their destination.

Usually she enjoyed the flights out to her tour locations, looking forward to meeting the people she'd

take on tours. There were always a few memorable
characters in each group, fascinating people with
interesting lives and philosophies. This last trip there
had also been the Texas Twins, whose pursuit of her
favours had been persistent beyond belief. She was
usually capable of dealing with one handsome male,
but coping with two identical copies had proved trying
in the extreme. In despair, she'd enlisted the help of a
friendly fifty-year-old, which had been a mistake.
He'd wanted a piece of the action and had
misinterpreted her plea for assistance.

The flights back home were very different from the
flights over. She was usually exhausted, ready for a
couple of weeks of relative rest, her own bed, her own
apartment. This time the feeling was more acute. She
was in no mood to deal with another handsome face.

The food arrived, served up on china dishes. A
white tablecloth was spread out on their tables. Wine
was poured into real glasses. Travelling first class had
definite advantages.

With a rueful look, Adam Cooper examined his
food, the shrimp cocktail, the Veal Parmesan, the
Bavarian cream dessert. 'Sometimes,' he said slowly,
'I have this craving for an ordinary, home-cooked
American meal. Roast beef, mashed potatoes, thick
gravy, and apple pie for dessert.'

'With ice cream on top,' Kate added impulsively.

He grinned. 'With ice cream on top.' He picked up
his knife and fork. '*Bon appétit.*'

Kate began to eat. The chicken was done Oriental
style, with soysauce, water chestnuts and crisp
vegetables. It was not bad. Just having a tablecloth
and a real plate to eat from made a difference.

Tomorrow night she'd be eating dinner at Ankie's
house in Haarlem, near Amsterdam. Ankie was a
schoolfriend from her days in Abidjan in the Ivory

Coast, where her father had been an engineer. She was now married and had a small baby. Kate was looking forward to spending a few days with her.

In her melodious voice, the flight attendant enquired if they wanted more wine. Adam Cooper held out his glass, Kate declined. They finished the meal, making no more than a few general remarks. Their dishes cleared away, they were offered coffee and liqueurs.

Adam Cooper leaned back in his chair, giving Kate an assessing look as he sipped his Grand Marnier. 'So, what do you do for a living that makes you travel so much of the time?'

The question had been expected. It was the one she'd answered untold times.

'I'm in the travel business. I'm one of four partners in a speciality travel agency. We develop, organise and lead tours to out-of-the-way places.' She wondered if she sounded like a recording.

'Such as Inner Mongolia?'

'Right. And my agency also rents villas, cottages, small hotels, inns, that sort of thing, in non-tourist areas. Many of our clients are well-known people, celebrities, actors, TV personalities who want to get away from everything, go to some place where they won't be recognised.'

'You must meet some interesting people.'

'I do. And what business are you in? No, let me guess.' She cocked her head and scrutinised him, examining his conservative suit, the tiny stripe of his shirt, the traditional tie, the short hair. He wore an expensive-looking watch. No rings or other jewellery. His leather briefcase was a classic. Not a banker or a politician; he'd be wearing a pin-stripe three-piece suit no matter what the temperature. Still, his whole appearance radiated conservatism. Private business. Some big corporation, most likely.

'You're not a banker or a politician.'

'No.' He seemed amused by her scrutiny.

'My guess is that you work for a big corporation. Computers, medical equipment, something like that.'

He grinned. 'Wrong. I'm in the hotel business.'

Well, not as wrong as he thought. The hotel business was very conservative. 'What sort of hotels?'

'I work for the Crown Hotel Corporation.'

Kate nodded. It was one of the major chains with hotels all over the world. 'Resort hotels, right?'

'Not all, but mostly. Ever stayed in one?'

'I don't believe so. Generally, I . . .' She stopped the flow of words and smiled. No sense in antagonising him.

'What were you going to say?'

She shrugged lightly. 'Never mind.'

His eyes narrowed slightly. 'I'd like to hear it.'

She observed him for a moment. 'All right. I was going to say that generally I stay away from chain hotels. They're all the same. Once you're inside you don't know whether you're in New York, Manila or Rio. I find that very depressing.'

He wasn't put out in the least. 'The tourists like it. They know exactly what they'll get. Like opening a can of Coca Cola. No surprises.'

'But it's so boring.'

'Not boring, *comforting*.' He smiled at her. 'Think about it. Not everybody is used to being in foreign places like you and me. For most people it's very exciting to go on a foreign vacation—they may do it only once in their lifetime. But it's also scary and threatening. Strange people, strange food, a strange language. A standard American hotel room feels like home. It's safe and comfortable. You can order hamburgers and french fries and apple pie. It's the perfect place to relax after you've ventured out into the wilds of all that foreignness all day.'

Kate frowned. 'You're right, of course. I just have such a different perspective myself, I don't always think of that.' She often took it for granted that her own life had been special. She was at home in the world. She knew the best places to shop in Hong Kong, Bangkok and Rome; the best restaurants in Nairobi, Cairo, Singapore, and none of them in the guide books. She could find her way in those cities and several others, without a map. She spoke fluent French and Malay and passable Thai and Swahili. Most of the people she dealt with, the agency's clients, were sophisticated individuals who'd done a fair amount of travelling already, for both pleasure and business. They came to the agency because they wanted something different—not just another trip, but an adventure.

Adam Cooper looked at her closely. 'You're obviously not the average tourist.'

Kate laughed. 'No.' She certainly wasn't. She had calluses on her legs and backside to prove it. Travelling around on horse and camel-back for three weeks probably wasn't what your average tourist considered a vacation. In Mongolia she and her clients had camped out in tents or slept in native *yurts*, gone without baths or showers for days and eaten very simple food. Obviously, this sort of thing was not for everybody, she appreciated that. The success of her own agency, however, indicated a growing interest for out-of-the-ordinary vacation adventures.

'You're dealing with a totally different aspect of the tourist industry than I do,' Adam Cooper was saying. 'I scout around for locations for new hotels, looking for places where everybody wants to go. Say Bali, for instance. I just came from there. We're thinking of building a hotel there.'

'One more hotel on Bali and the island will sink into the sea,' she couldn't help saying.

'At least the water is blue and warm,' he said, making her smile.

After the stop in Bombay, they were offered more drinks and then many of the passengers settled down either to sleep or watch the movie. Kate plugged in her earphones, found some agreeable music, and took a report from her briefcase. Roxanne had stuck a note on the front. 'Kate,' it read, 'let me know what you think of this when you get back.'

It was a report on a trip in Paraguay Roxanne had made with a friend, a try-out for a new addition to the agency's repertoire. She'd written a day-by-day account, with all the details of eating places, locally available food, places to sleep, and things to see, the weather, the people and whatever else she thought was noteworthy. Kate hadn't had a chance to read it, and she'd better do it now before she'd see Roxanne again in a few days. Roxanne was a good writer, with a dry, somewhat cynical sense of humour, and the report was entertaining reading.

Apparently not interesting enough to keep her conscious. The next thing Kate knew she was being gently nudged awake, and Adam Cooper was handing her the report, which must have slid off her lap and fallen on the floor.

'Sorry to wake you,' he said. 'But we're in Cairo. Better put your belt on and straighten your chair.'

She took the report from him, feeling foggy with sleep. 'Thanks.' She buckled her belt and raked her fingers through her hair. She felt as if he'd dragged her out of death. She didn't usually sleep so deeply on a plane. Sighing, she closed her eyes again and leaned back.

'Straighten your chair, Kate.'

She groaned and pushed in the button. The back of

chair pushed her upright and she opened her eyes
and sighed again. Sleeping was a lost cause now.
'What time is it?'

'Five-thirty in the morning, local time.'

It was still the dead of night as far as her biological
clock was concerned and, going by the way she felt,
her body quite agreed. 'After all the travelling I've
done, you'd think I'd get used to it,' she moaned. 'I
don't think I ever will. I feel like a wreck every time.'

'You look fine. A bit tousled, and rather seductive,
actually.'

'Flattery will get you nowhere,' she threatened
darkly.

He laughed. He looked perfectly fresh, as if he'd
had a restful night, a shower, breakfast, a multivitamin,
and was ready for the day. Some people always looked
like that no matter what the circumstances. She
couldn't stand it. Scowling, she rummaged through
her bag for a comb. She couldn't even get out of her
chair now that the plane was landing.

'Are you mad again?' Adam Cooper enquired
calmly. 'What did I do now?'

She'd found the comb. She clenched it as if it were a
weapon, feigning outrage. 'You just told me I looked
fine, seductive. At five-thirty in the morning, mind
you, after I've been asleep in a plane in my clothes.
It's the most flagrant lie I've ever heard. I happen to
have a suspicious nature, and it's at its best when I
meet someone like you.'

'Someone like me?' His eyebrows rose in mock
puzzlement.

She flashed him her sweetest smile. 'Charming,
flattering, too handsome for your own good. You
probably have a nice little wife tucked away in
Westchester. Not to speak of a couple of kids, a dog
and a cat.'

His eyes were laughing. 'I've no wife, in Westchester or anywhere else. Nor any kids, cats, dogs or other wildlife. I'm free, unattached and eminently eligible, I've been told.'

'Did I mention conceited? And eligible for what, may I ask?'

His eyes held hers. 'Whatever your heart desires.'

Here we go, thought Kate. 'My heart desires nothing.'

'Are you married?'

She laughed. 'Me? Married? You've got to be kidding. No one will have me. I'm out of the country seventy, eighty per cent of the time. Who'd mop the kitchen floor?'

'You have a point there. You could give up your career, of course. Stay home, mop the kitchen floor and take care of the kids.'

'That has been suggested to me on a number of occasions,' she acknowledged drily. She shook her head. 'No way. I'm looking for a man who'll give up his career and take care of the kids.'

'While you go riding around on camels in Mongolia.'

She grinned. 'You've got it. So much more fun than mopping the kitchen floor.'

The plane had landed and two men in flowing robes left the cabin. A cleaning crew came on board, quickly did their job and departed again. Two new passengers, a man and a woman, entered the cabin and settled themselves in their chairs. An hour after take-off they were served breakfast and the remaining hours of the flight passed easily enough. They made casual conversation, speaking mostly of their respective jobs, but Kate was aware of her own reserve, telling not too much, holding back. It was hard to ignore the undercurrents in their conversation and she wasn't immune to his considerable male attraction. The way he looked at her at times with those steady brown eyes gave her a weak feeling in her stomach. The knowledge of his tall, lean body so close to her was unnerving. When finally they landed in Amsterdam, she was relieved for more than one reason.

He was behind her as they went through the passport check and walked with her to collect their luggage. When her bags came first she said goodbye to him and he shook her hand. His hand was firm and cool, closing intimately over hers and holding it a little longer than was necessary.

'Goodbye, Kate. Have a good trip home.'

She smiled. 'Bye.' She extracted her hand and he let go, his mouth tilted in a smile.

Customs did not open her bags and she went through in only moments, seeing Ankie waving at her behind the glass partitions. She was wearing some wild outfit in turquoise and yellow and was hard to miss.

They hugged and kissed and laughed, telling each other how good it was to see each other again.

'Where's the baby?' Kate asked.

'At my neighbour's. It's his nap time and he would have been miserable if I'd brought him along. Come on, let's get out of this zoo.'

It was rainy and windy and Kate hugged her raincoat close to her. 'I always come at the wrong time of the year,' she complained.

'What do you mean? You don't like rain and wind? What else is there? They don't call this a frog country for nothing, you know.' Ankie's arm shot out to prevent Kate from crossing the road. 'Do me a favour and don't get run over by a truck while I'm watching.'

It was not until that night, after she'd gone to bed, that Kate realised that Adam had not tried to meet her again, had not asked for her address or her phone number. He'd merely said goodbye.

Well, that's a switch, she thought drily. She'd have refused to meet him again anyway. He wasn't her type. Too handsome, too conservative. She liked men who had a bit of pizzazz, who were slightly off-centre. Mr Adam Cooper was definitely not off-centre. He went straight down the middle of the road. A classic conservative. Square as a Rubik's cube. In no time he'd be talking about her moving in with him, about marriage, about her giving up her career to produce babies. Forget it. She turned over on her other side and pulled the covers up high around her shoulders.

'So,' she muttered to herself, 'why do you feel disappointed?'

CHAPTER TWO

NEW YORK smiled under a sunny summer sky when Kate arrived a few days later. Even the cabby who drove her home was cheerful. Kate looked like his wife, he informed her. She had red hair, too. Not as skinny as Kate though. She had a problem with her thyroid. Was close to two hundred pounds. Kate prayed she'd never have a problem with her thyroid.

The apartment was empty and quiet, the air warm and stuffy. Samantha wouldn't be back from the South Pacific until next week. Roxanne had moved out last month to share her life, temporarily at least, with a Lebanese immigrant who owned an Eastern-style nightclub in the City, belly dancers and all.

All four of them, Kate, Samantha, Roxanne and Becky, had started out together in a cheap, run-down apartment on the Lower East Side. When the business had started making profits, Kate and Samantha had moved to a better place. Roxanne had moved in with one of her lovers and Becky had married about the same time. There were three bedrooms in the apartment and Roxanne still shared it with them at times. With their many trips out of the country it did not make sense to have separate apartments.

Kate carried her suitcases to her bedroom, then went around opening windows. After a while she'd close them and turn on the air-conditioning. She sank down on the bed and let out a tired sigh. Well, first things first. Call the office and see if anything needed her immediate attention. She picked up the bedside phone and dialled.

'Janey? Hi, this is Kate. I just got back from Europe. Anything I should know before I collapse?'

'Nothing that can't wait till tomorrow. A man called for you today, though. Adam Cooper. Never heard of him.'

Involuntarily Kate straightened up. 'Adam Cooper? What did he say?'

'Nothing. Just that he wanted to speak to you. He said he'd call back.'

'All right. Well, I'll see you tomorrow then.' Kate hung up, frowning. How had he known where to reach her? She'd never mentioned the name of the agency, she was quite sure. Had he gone down the Yellow Pages to see which agency might be the one? He'd probably had a secretary figure it out. She shrugged. Well, never mind.

She got out of her clothes and had a long shower, luxuriating in the feel of the warm water pulsating down her body. Having closed the windows and turned on the air-conditioning, she crawled into bed.

Adam called again the next morning. Yesterday she'd thought long and hard on what course to take and decided that seeing him would not serve any purpose. He wasn't her type. She'd be setting herself up again for disappointment and she wasn't ready for that.

'Tell him I'm not here,' she told Janey.

'I already told him you were.'

'Tell him I left.'

'All right.' Janey sounded unhappy. 'When will you be back?'

'Nobody knows.'

Adam Cooper was not to be convinced. He called again an hour later, to be put off again. He called twice more.

His insistence exasperated Kate. 'Tell him I

suddenly had to go to the Azores, Alaska, any place. An emergency. Make something up.' She could tell the situation was getting to Janey. She was competent enough, but still young and quite inexperienced.

'I don't know if he'll believe me, Kate,' she said unhappily.

'Janey, you're a secretary. You're supposed to know how to lie in order to protect your boss. Didn't they teach you that in business school?'

'Maybe I missed it.'

'Well, give it a try. Practice makes perfect.'

She heard no more. When she left the office at five-thirty, Janey had already gone home.

She swung her bag over her shoulder and stepped out into the main lobby of the office complex.

'Hello, Kate.'

Kate stared at Adam, lounging against a grey marble post, mouth tilted in the now-familiar smile. Her heart made a ridiculous little leap, then changed into a nervous rhythm. She couldn't think of a thing to say.

'Surprise, surprise,' he mocked. 'Are you on your way to Alaska?'

Kate let out an exasperated sigh. 'What do you want, Adam?'

'What do you think I want? To start with, I wanted to talk to you. I called you half-a-dozen times today.'

'I was busy.'

'Too busy to pick up the phone and talk to me for a few minutes?'

She smiled sweetly. 'Yes.'

Why did he have to look so devastatingly handsome? Tall, lean, virile. He wore a grey suit, white shirt, grey striped tie. Not a wrinkle anywhere. What had he been doing all day?

'All right,' he said, moving towards her and taking

her arm, 'maybe you have time now. Let's go for a drink.'

'No thanks, I'm in a hurry.' She feigned a smile, trying to escape from his grip.

He didn't let go. Instead he moved in front of her, standing very close, both hands on her arms. He looked into her eyes, a gaze so intent, she couldn't avert her face. For a moment they stood in silence. And there was nothing but his eyes looking into the very depths of her and her heartbeat throbbed in her ears. She felt transfixed, hypnotised.

'Kate,' he said softly, 'if you truly can't come with me tonight, tell me.'

Her throat felt dry. 'I was just going home.' She felt dazed, disorientated, as if all the fight and determination had gone out of her and something else had taken over.

'Will you come with me for a drink?'

She nodded.

'My car is in the parking lot.'

He even had a car. Not many people living in Manhattan bothered with a car. There was never a place to park it and taking taxis was a lot easier.

Fifteen minutes later they were sitting in a small, cosy bar and Kate was wondering how he had managed to get her there. What was it about him that made her melt inside? What was it about the curve of his mouth, about the smile in those dark eyes? Magic promises . . . Of kisses of fire, touches of velvet. Promises of passion and pleasure, of laughter and loving. It was the most ridiculous thing that had ever happened to her.

Adam gave a crooked little smile. 'What are you thinking about?'

'I was wondering how you managed to get me here. I was determined not to come with you.'

'... y not?'

'Actually, I'm off men.'

'Temporarily, I hope.'

She shrugged. 'It's getting to be more trouble than it's worth. I had decided not to get involved for a while.'

'You sound bitter.'

'Not bitter, fed up. I've got this knack for attracting the wrong men.'

'What do you mean by wrong?'

'The kind of men who think too much of themselves. They're selfish. They want an instant relationship. They don't like my job because I travel too much. They want me to give up my career, live with them, marry them, whatever. They make all sorts of demands on me, assuming I'll be glad to do whatever it takes to pamper them. I'm tired of it.' She picked up her glass and took a swallow of sherry.

'All right,' he said slowly, 'I'll make you a deal. I solemnly promise you I won't ask you to give up your career, to live with me, or marry me, if you'll have dinner with me.'

'I thought we were just going out for a drink.'

'Since you're not doing anything, we might as well eat.'

'I have a feeling I'm about to fall into a trap.'

'I wouldn't know why. I'm making you a deal. No demands if you'll have dinner with me.'

'What about next time?'

'Next time will take care of itself.'

'That's what I was afraid of. No deal.'

He gave her a long, thoughtful look. 'All right,' he said at last, 'I won't ask you to give up your job, live with me, or marry me for the next three months.'

'Make it six.'

'You drive a hard bargain. And all that just for one dinner.'

But it wasn't just for one dinner, and he knew .

He took her to a wonderful French restaurant she'd never heard of. She wished she could have changed her clothes before going. Her blue shirtdress was perfectly respectable, but it was more suitable for the office than a restaurant. The customers were all dressed up for a night on the town, obviously all people with money to spend.

'Your office is in a good location,' Adam commented as they waited for their food. 'Good for lunch-time walk-ins, I expect.'

'Yes.' Kate frowned. 'How did you find me, anyway? You didn't ask for my address or phone number.'

He grinned. 'Bothered you, didn't it?'

'Never even thought of it until you called.'

'You're a bad liar.'

She ignored that. 'So, how did you find me? Did you have your poor secretary call all the travel agencies in the Yellow Pages?'

He shook his head. 'I had your office address and phone number before we even reached Cairo.'

She gave him a narrow-eyed look. 'How?'

'From the report you were reading. You fell asleep and it slipped off your lap. I picked it up and took the liberty to study the letterhead. Very simple.'

Of course! Why hadn't she thought of that! No wonder he hadn't asked her for a card, address, number, anything. And he'd known she'd expected him to. Well, that was one round for him. Two, actually. Here she was, sitting with him in this restaurant, against her better judgment. She felt suddenly manipulated. She *was* manipulated. Oh, for heaven's sake, she said to herself, don't get all heated up. Enjoy yourself. It's not going to last. He's not your type. Look at that suit, that tie.

The food tasted wonderful. She was hungry. Lunch had only been a sandwich and it had been a long time ago. She had to admit she was enjoying herself. Adam had a dry sort of humour she appreciated, and he talked about a number of subjects that surprised her. He hadn't grown up in a well-to-do-family, as she somehow had expected by his polished manner and exterior. He grew up in a small country town and had had, of all things, a cow named Minnie who'd once won a prize at a country fair. She couldn't quite visualise this handsome, sophisticated man in his superbly fitting suit as a boy polishing up cows' hooves and braiding a cow's tail. He was talking about this cow with total seriousness, telling her the details of its care and the things he did to practise before the fair.

'You think I'm making all this up,' he said, eyeing her narrowly.

Kate made no attempt to hide her laughter. 'Adam, it's the craziest thing I've ever heard of! You *shampoo* the tail of a cow and then you *braid* it? You've got to be kidding!'

'No, I'm not.' His face was perfectly straight, but there were laughing lights in his eyes. 'You braid the tail so it'll have curls when you take it out. Easier than using jumbo rollers.'

Kate choked on her strawberry tart. She dropped her fork, coughing and spluttering until the offending strawberry dislodged itself. She gulped down some water. Adam sat passively watching her.

'Sorry about that,' he said evenly.

Kate glowered at him. 'Your concern is touching. I could have died and you just sit there.'

'You were in no imminent danger. You were making impressive noises and you weren't turning blue.'

'Just a nice shade of beet red, I imagine. It clashes

with my hair; it's embarrassing.'

He grinned. 'That's what you get for not believing me. For such an educated, cosmopolitan woman, you have some serious gaps in your knowledge.'

A waiter hovered nearby with a coffee pot. 'Coffee?' he asked.

'Please.' Kate watched as he poured the steaming liquid into the white china cup.

'Would you care for a liqueur?' The man looked at them in polite enquiry. They both declined.

'I thought you liked Grand Marnier,' Kate observed.

'I do. But I've had a couple of drinks already and since I'm driving that'll have to do me for tonight.' He took a swallow of his coffee. 'Would you like to go somewhere else after this?'

'No thanks, I'd like to go home.'

He didn't argue. 'All right. Where's home? Or do I take you back to the office to pick up your car?'

'I don't own a car,' she said, knowing there was no way out now but to let him know her home address as well. Well, he would have found that out easily enough anyway.

It was not a long drive and he parked the car and walked her into the building. She smiled at the doorman, then turned to Adam.

'You don't need to go up with me. I'm quite safe. I . . .'

'Kate! You're back!'

Kate whirled around, John Sullivan, her neighbour, stood in front of her, grinning. He clutched a large bag of ice cubes to his chest and on his head perched a child's party-hat, a bright orange affair with streamers flowing from the pointed top.

'Hi, John, how are you?' She grinned. 'Dumb question. You're in fine shape, I can tell.' She turned o Adam, who stood silently watching them. 'Adam, his is John Sullivan, my neighbour. John, Adam ooper.'

'Sorry, can't shake your hand. It's frozen solid to his bag. I'm having a party. Come on up and join us, th of you.' He pushed the elevator button with his chin.

'Well, I'm not sure, John.'

'Of course you're sure. You love parties. I've tried to get hold of you all night, but all I got is that damn answering machine.'

Knowing John, she'd probably find some obscene message on it when she played the tape back later. But he was right, she did like parties and it was Friday night and still early.

She looked at Adam. 'Would you like to come? John's parties are famous; don't be fooled by the glamorous hat.'

'It's my birthday,' explained John. 'And I'll be highly offended if you refuse my invitation. Somebody made me a birthday cake the shape of a . . . well, never mind. You've got to see it.'

The elevator door slid noiselessly open. The three of them piled in. Kate pushed the button to their floor.

She couldn't fathom the expression on Adam's face. The left corner of his mouth tilted. 'I wouldn't miss it for the world.'

She couldn't believe he had actually accepted. It would be interesting to see how he would fit in. John was a successful commercial photographer and had a fascinating assortment of friends—people from the advertising world, publishing, artists and fashion models, even now and then a politician. The conversations were always animated, the food was always good, the parties never boring.

'I'll have to change,' she said to John. 'We'll be over in a short while.'

He looked her up and down, distaste in his eyes as he examined the blue dress. 'Please do. I didn't know you owned stuff like that. Wear something glamorous.'

Kate laughed. 'I'll see what I can find.'

John disappeared into his apartment and Kate found her key and opened the door to her own.

'Charming man,' Adam said drily as he followed her in.

'He likes to offend people for the fun of it. It takes some getting used to.' She went around turning on lamps, feeling suddenly awkward now that the two of them were alone in her apartment. She wished Samantha were home. He looked around the living-room.

'Nice place.'

'Thank you.' Good thing Roxanne wasn't living with them now or the place would have been a pigsty. 'Why don't you sit down? Would you like a drink?' She avoided looking at him directly.

He wandered slowly towards her, hands in his pockets, jacket pushed back. 'No, thanks.'

'Well, I'll just go and change then. I won't take . . .'

'Look at me, Kate.' He was standing in front of her. The door to her bedroom was behind her, blocking flight.

She smiled up at him sunnily in an attempt to hide the sudden feeling of trepidation. 'Yes?'

His hands came out to touch her hair. She jerked back. 'Don't touch me!'

'Why not?'

'Because I don't want you to!'

'Oh, but I think you do,' he said softly, a dark gleam of derision in his eyes. His hands smoothed her hair, then slid under it to the back of her neck in a gentle, sensuous gesture. His hands were warm against her skin and her heart began to thump painfully against her ribs. She couldn't move had she wanted to. His eyes held hers and his face slowly came closer until his mouth touched hers. His lips brushed lightly across her mouth—nothing more than a featherlike caress, yet it made her senses reel, and she protested against it with a rush of indignation. She pushed at his chest, anger mingling with the warm excitement that crept treacherously through her body.

His hands cradled her head, keeping it immobilised and against her struggles his mouth covered hers with a possessive fierceness that shook her to the core.

One part of her had wanted this, had secretly looked forward to the feel of his mouth on hers, his body pressed against hers. The expectation had been there from the moment they had met, the vibrations between them strong and undeniable. Yet another part of her screamed wildly in defence. How dare he do this! But the anger was drowned out by the warm tide of mindless delight that flooded her. She felt the strength drain out of her limbs, felt her mouth yielding to his, kissing him back. Her arms crept up around his back and held him.

When he finally released her, she found it hard to stand up on her trembling legs. For an endless moment he looked into her eyes, his mouth tilted at the corners.

'Tell me you didn't like that,' he taunted.

'I don't like your macho tactics,' she said huskily. 'And you don't impress me one bit.'

His eyes laughed into hers. 'No? Maybe I should try again.' He reached out for her, but she turned swiftly aside and avoided his hands. He laughed out loud, then lowered himself into a chair and stretched out his legs comfortably. 'Don't look so angry, Kate, it doesn't make you beautiful.'

'Get lost!' she said, stung by his laughter.

'Later, not yet. Go change into something glamorous.'

With as much calm dignity as she could muster, she opened the bedroom door, closed it behind her and turned the key. She let out a deep sigh. Oh, dear Lord, she thought, what did I get myself into?

She took off her dress, opened the wardrobe and scanned the contents. A long silky affair in greenish-turquoise caught her attention. The skimpy top was solid, but the skirt had a sprinkling of large shadowy flowers in orange and black. The colours and the cut were daring and exotic, not something that just anyone could wear. Kate took it off the hanger and slid it over her head, grinning at herself in the mirror. This should satisfy John. Adam would probably find it too flamboyant, but she didn't care. She liked her clothes bright and imaginative, although for the office she tried to keep her enthusiasms under control.

Adam gave her a thorough looking-over when she came back into the living-room, the expression in his eyes making her grit her teeth.

'Definitely glamorous,' was his verdict, and there was humour in his eyes. 'That should make your friend happy.'

Was he laughing at her? She wondered what he himself thought of the dress. She felt a prick of irritation. He definitely had the power to make her feel on the defensive.

'Let's go,' she said coolly, opening the front door.

It was well after two when Kate decided it was time to go. She'd done her share of talking and laughing, and had probably had a drink too much. She went in search of Adam.

'I think I've had it,' she announced when she found

him alone on the balcony, staring out over the river. 'Why are you here all alone?'

He looked down at her, one eyebrow raised. 'Because I like it here.'

'Didn't you like the party?' She had noticed that he had not mingled much, seemingly content to hover on the edges of the activities, observing the goings-on with mild amusement. A few females had gravitated towards him, attracted by his looks, but he'd managed to lose them and for a while he'd been in conversation with John. His eyes had followed her around the room as she made the rounds talking and laughing with the other guests. It had made her faintly uneasy and she wasn't sure why.

'The party was fine. I'm not a very social animal, unfortunately.' The tilt of his mouth indicated that he wasn't regretful in the least.

'Why did you come then?'

'Because you were here.'

She smiled sweetly. 'I'm flattered. Well, I'm going now. I wanted to say good night and thank you for dinner. You don't have to leave because I'm going.'

'But I will. It's late.'

They said goodbye to John and walked out into the hall.

'I'll call you tomorrow,' said Adam, kissing her lightly in front of her door. He made no attempts to come in with her and she was ridiculously relieved. Somewhere in the back of her mind she was beginning to fear that Adam Cooper was not a man she could handle easily.

She had barely taken off her clothes when a knocking on her door reverberated through her apartment. Wrapping her robe around her she went up to the door.

'Who is it?'

'It's me, Adam.'

She took a deep breath. 'Adam! I want to go to sleep!'

'So do I! Open the door, I need to call the police.'

'The police?' Without further thought she took the chain off the door and unlocked it. 'What's wrong?'

'My car is out of commission,' he said as he stepped inside. 'I wonder if I could sleep on your couch.'

She could feel the anger rise hot inside her. 'So original,' she said sarcastically. 'What is it? Is the battery dead? Did the steering wheel fall off? Did somebody steal your gas?'

'They stole my tires.'

She gaped at him. 'You're not serious!'

'I'm deadly serious. All four of them taken off. Go down and see for yourself if you don't believe me. This may be a good neighbourhood, but it's still New York. And by the way, the lock on the door downstairs is broken. I walked right back in.'

Kate sighed. 'Oh, great. Well, you'd better call the police.'

'For whatever good it will do.'

She left him to it and went into the bathroom to take off her make-up and brush her teeth. She was suddenly very tired. She shouldn't have stayed so late, but it had been a good party and she had enjoyed herself.

And now Adam was here in her apartment, staying the night. He could go home in a taxi, but it was easier to just let him stay here for the few hours that remained of the night. She felt helpless, angry, and she didn't quite know why. She hadn't wanted to see him again and here he was staying the night. How had it all happened? Where was this going to end? She slammed the bedroom door as she came out ten minutes later.

Adam lay stretched out on the couch, legs sticking out. 'I thought you'd gone to bed,' he said.

'You can sleep in Samantha's room,' she offered. 'That door over there. The bed is probably stripped, but there are sheets in the closet next to the bathroom. There are towels, too. Help yourself. I'm going to bed.' She turned abruptly. 'Good night.'

'Hey, wait a minute!' He came to his feet in one smooth, flowing movement. 'What is the matter with you?'

'Nothing is the matter with me. I'm tired. I started out the day not wanting to see you, then agreeing to a drink, then getting suckered into having dinner with you and now you're sleeping in my apartment. I feel manipulated! You've forced your way into my life, into my apartment, and I don't like it! Well, I can't physically throw you out, can I? So I'll just have to accept the fact, but I don't have to like it.'

'What are you afraid of?'

'I'm not afraid of anything! I'm mad!'

'Why are you so angry with me all the time? Why all this misdirected emotion?'

'Misdirected emotion? What the hell are you talking about?'

'I think you're hiding. I think you're afraid of what you really might be feeling for me.'

'Of all the outrageous, arrogant things I've ever heard! I . . .'

He didn't let her finish. In two long strides he was with her, pinning her against the wall, kissing her mouth, her eyes, her neck with a fiery passion that left her limp in his arms. She had no defence against his onslaught, feeling her blood rush like fire through her as he slid his hands inside her robe and stroked her breasts.

Then abruptly he stepped back. 'That's what I

mean,' he said, his voice low and quiet. 'You can't
fight it. Not with anger, not with words, not with your
body. It's there and you'd better admit it to yourself.'

Her knees were shaking. She felt hot with anger—at
herself for feeling the way she did, at him for having
this terrible power over her. 'Wouldn't you like that?'
she said acidly, clutching the robe across her breast.
'One more female who's fallen for your handsome
face. Your arrogance is stunning!'

His eyes narrowed and his jaw grew rigid. 'Look,
lady,' he said, the anger in his voice only barely
controlled, 'I don't have to take this. I don't need your
anger or your immature obsessions and hangups. I
don't know what possessed me to go after you in the
first place.' He turned on his heel, walked out the
front door and slammed it behind him.

She hung weakly against the wall, staring at the
closed door. Then, with shaking knees, she went back
into her bedroom and crawled into bed, hugging the
sheet close around her.

Good riddance, she thought. He won't be back. But
his words wouldn't leave her alone and they kept
repeating themselves in her tired mind. *You can't fight
it—not with anger, not with words, not with your body.*
The frightening thing was, she knew he was right.

Despite the late hour and her fatigue, she barely
slept. She'd sink away into a restless slumber, then
float back into dazed consciousness, wondering about
Adam. Had he been able to get a taxi to take him
home? It wouldn't have been easy at that late hour.
Maybe he'd had to walk. She visualised him walking
the streets of New York, block after block. Maybe
he'd got mugged. Maybe he lay bleeding in the street
somewhere. Maybe he was dead. It would all be her
fault. Her imagination was working overtime. She was
beginning to feel worse and worse. At six she gave up

the struggle and dragged herself out of bed. She took a shower, dressed in white shorts and a jungle print shirt and made a pot of coffee.

After two cups of coffee she took the elevator down and went into the parking lot of the building to look for Adam's car. It was where he had parked it last night, minus four wheels. Of all the cars there, they'd picked his. What would he do now? He'd have to come back for it. Put new wheels on it, something.

She went back inside. The doorman looked at her with a worried frown. 'Your friend's car?'

She nodded.

'That's the second time in the last month,' he announced.

'The second time?' She looked at him, aghast.

'You were gone. They took the wheels of Mr Cannon's Ferrari. Must have been the same thugs.' He nodded at Adam's car. 'Did he call the police?'

'He did last night, when he found out. I don't know what they said. If they come later, would you mind giving me a buzz? I don't know when my friend will be back.'

'I'll keep an eye out.'

Kate went back upstairs. All was quiet in John's apartment. She wondered at what time the last of his guests had departed. When she and Adam had left, the party had still been in full swing.

An hour later the doorman buzzed her. 'The police are here, and your friend, too. He has new wheels.'

'Thank you very much. I'll be right down.'

She stayed in the lobby watching the procedures from a side window. Two police officers examined the car, took down information, and departed. Four new wheels lay on the ground. Adam got out the jack and cranked up one side of the car and proceeded to attach one of the wheels.

Her heart galloping nervously, Kate went outside.

He didn't see her approach, his eyes intent on what he was doing. He was wearing jeans and a black T-shirt. He looked different from the formally dressed man she knew. The shirt stretched tightly across his back and chest and his bare arms were brown and strong, the muscles rippling as he lifted the second wheel into position.

'Hi,' she said.

He looked up, his face emotionless. 'Good morning.' He turned his attention back to the wheel, tightening bolts with swift, efficient turns, ignoring her.

She watched him in silence as he took down the jack and moved it to the front, cranking up the left side. Without a word, still ignoring her, he attached the third wheel and swiftly moved to the fourth.

If she didn't say something, he'd be in his car, driving off in a few more moments. And he wouldn't come back, she knew that.

'Would you like to come up for some breakfast when you're done?' she asked.

'I've eaten, thanks.' His voice was curt and he didn't look at her. He straightened and put away the jack, slamming the trunk lid down with finality.

Her hands were clammy and she wiped them on her shorts. 'Adam, can we talk?'

'I haven't got time, I'm late as it is.'

'Please, Adam, don't do this to me!'

One eyebrow rose in question. 'What am I doing to you?'

'You're deliberately making it difficult for me.' She closed her eyes briefly. 'I want to apologise for last night.'

His eyes looked into hers for a long moment. 'All right, apology accepted.' Then he looked at his watch and frowned. 'Could I come up and use your phone?'

'Sure.' She looked at his hands. 'You might want to wash your hands, too.'

'Yes, I suppose that's not a bad idea.'

They rode the elevator in silence. Once inside she gave him a clean towel and showed him the bathroom. Unsure of what to do, she went into the kitchen and poured herself another cup of coffee and stared out of the window, sipping it slowly.

Below her simmered the city in the summer heat. Grey buildings, rooftops cluttered with vents and chimneys and TV antennae. Here and there balconies sported containers of flowers, bright splashes of colour in the depressing vastness of drab concrete.

She turned when she heard Adam behind her. He gestured towards her cup. 'Is there more of that, or do you have to make it?'

'The pot is hot. I'll pour you some.' She opened the cupboard above the sink, her hand hesitating as she reached out for a mug. Samantha's mug was sitting there right in front. The mug Roxanne had given her last year after a terrible fight that had gone on for days. NOBODY'S PERFECT. BUT I COME CLOSE it read in rainbow colours. She took it down quickly before she could change her mind, and poured coffee into it.

'Here you go,' she said, handing it to him. 'There's a phone in the living-room, or you can use the one in Samantha's bedroom.'

'Thanks.' He turned and strode out of the kitchen.

The sounds of the quick clicks as he punched in the number reached her from the living-room.

'Sue? This is Adam. I'm sorry I'm late. I had trouble with my car.' A moment's silence as he listened. 'No, no. It's fixed. I'm still coming. Tell him I'll be there in about forty-five minutes and we'll go to the museum to see the dinosaurs, or wherever else he wants to go.' Another pause. 'It's no problem, Sue. See you in a little while.' With a firm click the receiver was replaced. Kate stared down into the street below. A police car slowly cruised by. Who was Sue? Who was Adam taking to see the dinosaurs? A child? Maybe Sue was his ex-wife and he was picking up his son for the weekend. But on the plane he'd denied having children. Maybe Sue was his sister. Maybe he was taking his nephew out for the day. Maybe he'd been lying about having kids. The thoughts whirred in her head at alarming speed.

Adam came back into the kitchen, pulled out a chair and straddled it. He took a mouthful of coffee, put the cup down and stared at it. After a moment he raised his eyes to hers and the sadness in their depths shook her to the core.

'I'm not so perfect myself, either,' he said.

CHAPTER THREE

KATE's heart contracted at the pain in his voice. She stared at him, not knowing what to say, not knowing what he was referring to. The sharp edges of her suspicions softened as she gazed at the handsome face that suddenly looked so vulnerable. It only lasted for a moment.

He stood up abruptly, his face expressionless again. 'I'm free tonight. Would you like to go out?' His voice was businesslike and under control.

Kate took a deep breath. 'How about coming here?' she said impulsively. 'I'll fix us something to eat. We see enough restaurants and hotel coffee shops while we're travelling.'

A slow smile lit up his face. 'I'd like that.'

'Good. How about seven?'

'Fine.' He glanced at his watch. 'I'd better go now. I'll see you tonight.'

After he had left, Kate poured herself another cup of coffee. 'Oh, my,' she muttered to herself. 'Here I go again.'

Still, a sense of excitement took hold of her as she planned the dinner. As she considered all the exotic meals she could cook, a memory of Adam staring wistfully at his tray of food in the airplane came unbidden to her mind. *'Sometimes I have this craving for an ordinary home-cooked American meal. Roast beef, mashed potatoes . . .'*

She looked at her watch, grabbed her purse and rushed out of the door. In the supermarket she loaded her trolley with the best oven roast she could find, potatoes, apples, the creamiest richest vanilla ice-cream. She bought a bottle of wine, which probably wouldn't have been part of the home-cooked American meals he remembered, but he probably wouldn't mind that little deviation. She couldn't quite see going to the extreme of serving him milk with his dinner in the great American tradition.

With Stephane Grappelli accompanying her on the violin, she spent the afternoon happily cooking, making apple pie from scratch, which she hadn't done for years. Such an extravaganza, she thought, and all for a man. I must be crazy. Rushing back and forth between kitchen and dining-room, she set the table with her best white tablecloth, dishes and glasses. Twice more she raced out to the shops to get something she had forgotten—coffee, and a big bunch of daisies to decorate the table.

Well, I'm sure getting my exercise today, she told herself as she hurried down the street with the daisies in her arms. It was hot and the perspiration was running down her back and between her breasts and her hair was wet. New York in July was the pits. Why was she running around outside like this? She could have been inside in her nice cool apartment all day, lazing on the sofa with a good book, instead of going through all these contortions to please a man. Kate, my friend, you're doing it again. When are you going to learn? Probably never, she answered herself.

Everything under control, she had a shower and washed her hair. Now the big question, she thought as she stood in front of her wardrobe. What does one wear for an affair such as this? Something homey and old-fashioned and conservative. Adam should like that. She grinned. Whatever it was, it was definitely not something she had in her wardrobe. Frowning, she scanned the row of brightly coloured clothes. Forget it, she thought. You'll have to find it somewhere else.

Somewhere else was Samantha's wardrobe. She and Samantha were the same size, but there all similarities ended. Samantha was blonde, blue-eyed, and loved lacy, frilly, feminine clothes, sometimes bordering on the prim and prissy. It didn't take Kate long to find something—a fitted dress, pearly grey with a small, white lace collar and pearl buttons down the front. She held it out and examined it, shaking her head. 'My God, Samantha,' she muttered, 'where do you find this stuff?' Of course, Samantha said the same thing about Kate's clothes, which she considered much too extravagant in design and colour.

Kate took the dress to her bedroom and tried it on, chuckling at the sight of herself in the mirror. Perfect, just perfect. Now for her hair. She'd put it up in a bun, not too severe though, she didn't want to overdo it. There had to be limits. Severe proved a problem with all the curls that kept escaping, but it did look a lot more demure than her usual loose curly hair style. The total picture was rather interesting. She hardly recognised herself.

When Adam arrived she was ready. The smell of roasting meat permeated the apartment and the stereo emitted gentle, cultured waves of classical piano music. He looked her over for a moment before entering, his eyes narrowing as he took in the prim dress. Then his eyes met hers and it was hard to hide her laughter.

'Come in, come in.'

'Thank you.' He stepped inside, handing over the bottle of wine he had in his hand. He wore pale grey slacks with a razor-sharp crease down each leg, a fitted white shirt, a tie and a blue blazer.

'It smells wonderful in here,' he commented.

'Good. I hope you're hungry.'

He grinned. 'Ravenous. All I had for lunch was a hotdog.'

A hotdog? Kate wondered. Oh, he'd taken a child to see the dinosaurs. No wonder. 'Dinner will be ready in about half an hour,' she said. 'Would you like a drink first?'

'You have Scotch?'

'I do. On ice?'

'Please.'

'Sit down, I'll be right back.'

She rushed to the kitchen, checked the boiling potatoes and the temperature on the meat thermometer stuck in the roast. She wondered how he liked his meat—rare, medium, well-done? She'd stick to medium. Asking him now would give it all away.

She filled a highball glass with ice and splashed whisky over it. A shot glass for measuring was nowhere to be found. She poured some wine for herself and carried the glasses to the living-room.

'Feel free to take off your jacket,' she invited. 'And that tie. I don't normally entertain men who wear ties. They make me nervous,' she improvised.

'The ties or the men?'

'Both.'

'I wonder why.'

'Ties make me think of nooses. I once developed a theory about men wearing ties, but I don't think I should tell you. You might walk out of the door again and then what would I do with the dinner I spent all day cooking?'

'All day? I'd better be prepared to like it.'

Her smile was a sugar-coated threat. 'You'd better. And how was your day with the dinosaurs?' She sipped her wine, eyeing him expectantly over the rim of her glass. Would he tell her about the boy?

'Educational.' She could almost see the shutters go down and he frowned. 'How did you know . . .?'

'You mentioned it on the telephone this morning. I was in the kitchen and I couldn't help but hear you. Do you often visit the dinosaurs? You don't seem the type. I had you pegged as a Saturday tennis player.'

'I do that too, when I get a chance. What about you? You play tennis?'

'Yes.' Obviously he wasn't going to tell her about the boy. Well, it was none of her business. 'I've played tennis since I was eight.'

'How good are you?'

'Very, very good,' she bragged with a bright smile. 'And I'd better get into the kitchen before something burns.'

'Can I help?'

His offer was a good sign. 'I'm not sure, but you can keep me company. Bring your glass.'

In the kitchen she tied on an apron, an orange affair with brown kangaroos jumping all over it—a present from an Australian friend. Usually she didn't bother with aprons, but since she was wearing Samantha's dress, she'd better protect it from disaster.

Adam's face lit up when she removed the roast from the oven.

'Don't tell me,' he said.

She smiled sedately. 'A real home-cooked American meal. Roast beef, mashed potatoes, peas. And apple pie for dessert, with ice-cream. Are you surprised?'

'You didn't seem a roast-beef-mashed-potato girl to me,' he said, obviously puzzled. 'How did you . . .?' He grinned. 'I'm beginning to sound like a recording.'

'You mentioned it on the plane.'

He nodded slowly. 'I remember now. Very observant, aren't you?'

'I try.' She took the roast out of the pan and poured

the drippings into a saucepan to make the gravy.
'What had you expected me to feed you?'

'Anything from a carry-out deli sandwich to
something *haute cuisine*.' He grinned. 'But certainly
not roast beef and mashed potatoes.'

The look in his eyes warmed her and a soft, curling
sensation began deep in her stomach.

'It's the only thing I knew for sure you'd like.'

'And you went through all this trouble to cook it.
Let me help. Shall I mash the potatoes?'

'If you would, please. The masher is in that drawer.
Milk and butter in the fridge. You want an apron?' She
didn't want to be responsible for mashed potato
splatters all over his pristine white shirt front. He had
taken off his jacket, but the tie was still in place.

'I think I can manage to do this without making too
much of a mess.' He opened the drawer and took out
the masher.

The gravy made, the potatoes mashed, they carried
everything to the table. She lit the candles, and poured
the wine. The daisies smiled innocently in the soft
light.

She had certainly outdone herself, Kate had to
admit to herself. The food was superb and it pleased
her to see Adam relish every bite.

'Do you cook for yourself when you're home?' she
asked, after they'd retreated to the living-room with
coffee and pie.

'Sometimes, but nothing complicated. I'm not much
of a cook. I often eat out, mostly business. This apple
pie is better than my mother's and I've never said that
to another woman.' There was laughter in his eyes and
Kate smiled back.

'Why, thengk you, suh,' she sang in her best
southern belle imitation.

There was the sound of a key in the door, then it

opened. Surprised, Kate got up from her chair, seeing Samantha staggering in lugging two pink suitcases. Her blonde hair billowed in soft, shiny waves around her face and the big blue eyes were bright with pleasure.

'Kate! I'm so glad you're home!' She came up to Kate and hugged her. Kate grinned.

'Hi, Sam, good to see you again. It's been ages.'

Samantha sighed. 'Yeah.' Then she frowned, looking at Kate, head tilted. 'You look weird. For one thing, you're wearing my dress.'

'Do you mind?'

'No, of course not. I must thought you'd drop dead before you'd put on something of mine. I can see why. It doesn't look like you.' She giggled. 'My God, you look like a virgin school marm. What smells so good in here?' Her eyes widened in surprise as she noticed Adam on the couch. 'Oh goodness, I didn't realise you had company. Leave it to me to come home at the wrong time.'

Kate made introductions. It was easy to tell from Samantha's expression that she was duly impressed with Adam, which did not come as a surprise. He was certainly much more her type than Kate's. Then Samantha's eye caught the apple pie.

'Did you make that? Is there any more?'

'Six more pieces. Want a couple?' Samantha had a legendary sweet tooth and a dentist's bill to prove it. Yet despite all the desserts and cakes and cookies she devoured she never seemed to gain an ounce.

Samantha grinned. 'Maybe even three, but I need to get out of these clothes first.' She disappeared into her bedroom, Adam gallantly carrying her suitcases for her.

After Samantha had had her piece of pie, she retired to bed, saying she was bushed. Adam pulled Kate next to him on the couch and deliberately began taking out the pins in her hair.

'What do you think you're doing?' she protested.

'I don't like it up like that.' He ran his fingers through her hair to loosen the curls.

She moved away from him. 'Don't you think that's just a little bit presumptuous? Telling me how to wear my hair?'

'Then we're even. You told me you don't like my tie.'

'I didn't say that. Actually, it's a very nice tie.' She reached out and fingered it. 'Nice colour. Silk, too.'

He grabbed her hand and drew her closer, the other hand trailing through her hair. 'Nice colour. Silky, too.' He laughed into her eyes and she couldn't keep her face straight.

'You're so clever.'

'I'm glad you finally realised it.'

'And arrogant and conceited. I can't stand arrogant, conceited men.'

'Show me,' he whispered, putting his arms around her. His mouth brushed her lips. 'Show me you can't stand me.'

She turned her head, trying to avoid his mouth, but with one hand he took her head and held it in place. With his body he pushed her down on the couch until she couldn't move an inch one way or the other. She squirmed beneath him, then stopped, realising this was not the way to keep him, or herself, calm. The intimacy of the close contact made her light-headed with feverish sensations. She lay very still, staring up into his laughing face, the throbbing of her pulse filling the silence.

Slowly, very slowly, his mouth came down on hers again, brushing seductively across her closed lips, tantalising, teasing, until they parted. Her body relaxed against him and no amount of self-control could fight the feelings his mouth and hands evoked in her. It wasn't fair that she was so at his mercy, but as long as that was the case, she might as well enjoy it.

There was fire in his kiss, promising greater joys and wilder delights and she responded with dangerous eagerness, yet for these few magical moments she didn't care. Her arms crept up around him, her hands flattening against the strong, muscled back.

After an endless time, he raised his head. His eyes glittered darkly. 'Tell me again I'm arrogant and conceited.'

For a moment she couldn't manage a coherent thought. She took in a deep breath, fighting for composure. It took an effort to come back to earth and formulate an answer. 'On second thoughts I think I'll take that back. On one condition.'

'And what is that?'

'That you let me go.' Please, please let me go, she prayed silently, before I do something irredeemably stupid.

'Not yet. First tell me your theory about men who wear ties.'

'You don't want to hear.'

'I asked you.'

'You're not going to like it.'

'If I get mad and walk out, at least you're not left with your dinner. I think I ate most of it.'

'Okay, you asked for it. But let me sit up. It's a long story.'

'All right,' he relented, taking the weight of his body off her.

She straightened the dress. 'Look what you did. You wrinkled Samantha's dress. What am I going to tell her?'

'That you were ravished on the couch, and don't change the subject.'

'What were we talking about?'

'Ties. Men who wear ties.'

'Okay, let me think.' She frowned in a pretence of concentration. 'Men who wear ties when not strictly necessary are conventional types who are afraid to be on their own and use their own judgement,' she began. 'They need the security of a leash, so to speak. They prefer other people to tell them what to do and where to go and they show little initiative. They do not like to think and make decisions on their own. They're afraid to take risks and prefer to travel the trodden path, so there won't be any surprises. The tie, really, is a symbolic leash, or even a noose.' Satisfied with her impromptu lecture, she looked at him expectantly.

'I think you should write a book about that theory,' he said, not in the least put out. 'There's big money in pop psychology these days.'

'The problem is I don't have a degree in psychology to display on the cover,' she said regretfully.

'You seem to be doing all right without one.' The mockery in his voice was hard to miss. 'Any more theories you'd like to share?'

'Not at the moment.' She smiled sedately, tucking her hair behind her ears. 'Tell me, am I right?'

His eyes held hers and a slow smile spread across his face. 'You'll have to find that out for yourself,' he said softly, trailing a finger seductively along her jawline.

She moved away from his exploring finger. 'I may not have the time.'

'No? How long will you be in New York?'

'I leave next week Sunday.'

'Where are you going?'

'Oh,' she said lightly, 'I'm going to spend a few weeks with the Barbarians.' She grinned at his quizzical expression. 'Berbers, I mean. Comes from the Latin *barbarus*, which means barbarian.'

'There are millions of them all over North Africa. Where exactly are you going?'

'Morocco. The Atlas Mountains. I'm leading a group of ten people. We're going to stay in a mountain village with a tribe of Berbers.'

'I don't believe it for a minute.'

'You think I'm lying?'

'You're telling me a story.'

She couldn't help laughing. 'It's true! I've done it for the last three years with the same tribe, in the same village.'

He looked at her narrow-eyed, and Kate, still laughing, held up her hand. 'Swear to God. They even wrote about it in the *New York Times* last year. Got my picture in the paper and everything. Not that you'd recognise me, of course. I was all swaddled up in a dark robe and a head-dress with a hundred bangles and you could only see my eyes.'

'I must have missed it,' he said drily.

'Entirely possible, isn't it? You were probably in the Fiji islands or some place like that. Planning a super-de-luxe hotel with an Olympic-size swimming pool, jogging track, tennis courts . . .'

He ignored the jibe. 'Berbers are nomads and they aren't known for their friendly attitude towards strangers.'

'They all *used* to be nomads. In Morocco a lot of them have become sedentary and live in mountain villages now. And believe it or not, some of them are even friendly to strangers.'

It was a very special tour, with participants carefully prepared. They lived just like the Berbers, dressed like them, ate their food, worked with them as best they could. They were the guests of the villagers, participating in the village life as much as they were allowed. Living in such primitive circumstances was an experience people never forgot. Some even wanted to repeat it. Two of the men that had participated two years ago had signed up again this time.

'And you, a woman, are in charge? Berbers, I believe, aren't favourably disposed to Western women and all the decadence they personify.'

'Oh, don't worry! My life and virtue, not to speak of my liver, are well-protected by a two-hundred-and-twenty-pound ex-wrestler.' Which was a slight exaggeration. Dick was possibly one-hundred-and-eighty pounds and no wrestler as far as she knew, but he looked like one, which counted for something. He was also in his sixties, spoke Berber and, having studied the Berbers for countless years as an anthropologist, was well-versed in their culture and habits. Without Dick, whom she'd had considerable difficulty convincing her expedition was a good idea, she could never do this tour.

'Your life, virtue and *what*?' Adam asked. 'Did you say *liver*?'

'The Berbers view the liver sort of like we do the heart. The seat of love and good health. Still don't believe me? I've got lots of neat little tidbits of inside knowledge. I may not know much about braiding cows' tails, but I know more about Berbers than you'll ever want to know.'

Adam rolled his eyes, and Kate laughed, then jumped up. 'You want some more coffee?'

'No, thanks. Sit down, relax.' He reached for her hand and pulled her down again. 'You don't ever sit still for very long, do you? All night you've been jumping up and down and racing back and forth.'

'I was born that way. Ruined a brand-new crib trying to get out. Tore at the thing so long that finally it collapsed. Nobody believes it, but it's true. They couldn't keep me in a playpen either. I'd scream bloody murder and bang my head on the edge so hard I'd be black and blue. People thought I was a victim of child abuse. Very embarrassing for my parents.'

He was still holding her hand. 'Did you always talk so much, too?'

'Yeah, even before I could speak.'

He grinned. 'Oh, shut up, Kate. Calm down.'

'I can't.'

'I'll give you a little help.' He leaned forward, took her face in his hands and kissed her. A flare of warmth raced through her, which did nothing to calm her down. His mouth was firm, but gentle, and her lips parted under the invitation. When she got a little more excitement than she was prepared to deal with for the moment, she drew away.

'That was supposed to relax me?' she asked with mild sarcasm.

'It didn't work?' He looked pleased with himself.

'No, it makes me want to run even faster and farther.'

'I wonder why.'

'Kissing is dangerous. My friend Amy in third grade told me so. She said if you kiss too often and too long, you get babies. And she probably knew. She knew everything else. She got straight As in school.'

'A real scientist, I can tell. And you're not ready for babies, I take it.'

'I wouldn't know what to do with them. Maybe when I'm big.'

'And when will that be?'

'Oh, not until I'm thirty-three. At least. And what about you? Are you ready for babies?'

'I think so. I'm big now, you see.'

'Have you never been married?'

He shook his head. 'No.'

'Why not?'

'I was married to my career. No time, no energy.'

'And now you have?'

'My priorities are shifting. I think I'd like to be married now, have a family. I'm tired of being alone.'

She wondered how often he'd actually been alone, how many affairs he'd had. Not that that was the same, of course. She gave him her sweetest smile. 'That makes you doubly dangerous.'

He shook his head. 'Since when don't women want to get married any more?'

'Since they got careers, money, freedom. We don't need to be married any more.'

He ran a finger slowly down her nose. 'Maybe I'll get lucky.'

She smiled sunnily. 'Maybe you will. Somewhere out there must be a girl who's dying to marry a handsome, charming, eligible . . .'

She didn't get a chance to finish her sentence. His mouth came down on hers with fierce possession. His arms clamped around her, holding her close. He kissed her until she was nothing but a bundle of shivering nerves and all reason had departed on wings of delight. His hands were doing wonderful things to her body and she didn't have the strength to push him away. After he had well and truly aroused her, he stood up from the couch and grinned down at her.

'Kate, my girl,' he said slowly, 'you have a lot of ideas and opinions, but you're not fighting me very hard, are you? If you mean what you say, you'd better watch out.' He picked up his blazer from the chair and pushed his arms into the sleeves.

Kate sat up, raking her hands through her hair, fighting a confusing mixture of emotions. 'Are you leaving?'

'You want me to stay?'

'No!'

He laughed. 'Scared, aren't you?'

'Not a bit. It's one of my rules not to sleep with men who wear ties to social affairs.'

'You should try it some time. You might just enjoy it.' He came back towards her, bent down and kissed the top of her head. 'Thanks for a wonderful dinner. Good night.' He turned and crossed the room, opened the door and was gone.

She sat still on the couch for a few more minutes, waiting, hoping somebody might have stolen his wheels again.

Monday afternoon Kate was wrestling herself through a mountain of paperwork at the office when Samantha came fluttering in and tossed a magazine on her desk.

'Read this!' she ordered, whirling around and dashing out again. Kate picked the journal up and glanced at it. It was the monthly publication of the Hotel Management Association. A note stuck to the glossy cover. *Thought you might like to read this*, it said in Samantha's flowery handwriting. *Page 42. Wow!*

A full-page photograph of Adam greeted her as she found the indicated place and her heart gave a small but undeniable leap. It was an arresting picture, the angle accentuating the square chin and the strong lines of his face. The mouth was unsmiling and the eyes slightly narrowed in intense concentration. There was something hard and ruthless in his expression, something she hadn't seen in the face of the live man she knew.

The picture accompanied a profile of Adam's career, and she read quickly through the article, mentally highlighting the various words used to describe his career, character and performance. *Harvard Business School ... ambitious ... talented ... highly motivated ... exceptional abilities ... impressive record ... major contributions ... brilliant insights. ...* She tossed the magazine down, letting out a long, slow breath. Phew! A wonder boy, huh?

The phone rang, leaving her no time to contemplate what she had just read. Moments after she had finished the phone call, Janey brought in a package that had been delivered for her. Puzzled, she opened the card that accompanied it. *My sincere appreciation for the best meal I've had in months, Adam.* It was an oblong box, not very big, and she ripped off the paper in eager anticipation. It was an old, dark blue case that held a pair of old-fashioned round granny glasses. For a moment she stared at the glasses in total mystification, then opened the folded note that had laid on top. *I thought something was not quite right about your costume Saturday night, but couldn't put my finger on it. When I came across these yesterday, I knew what it was.*

Kate laughed out loud, seeing her reflection in the shiny lenses. There was not a scratch on them. She put them on to find they were ordinary glass, probably put in new just for her. Rummaging in her purse, she found her hand mirror and looked at herself for a long moment. Oh, Adam, she thought, grinning at herself, maybe there's more to you than I thought!

Three nights that week they went out, and all three nights he brought her home, kissed her nearly senseless, and departed. He was playing a game with her, proving a point. Unfortunately, it was working: he was driving her crazy. She had no defences. She was hopelessly attracted to him and she couldn't fight it.

They were having a wonderful time together, going out to eat, to a concert, to an art gallery that had a special exhibit of Haitian art she'd wanted to see. One evening they stayed at the apartment on Samantha's invitation. She'd cooked an elaborate meal and had also invited Roxanne and Becky and her husband. They weren't often home in New York at the same time and they enjoyed an evening like this when they were. Roxanne's Lebanese lover had been unable to come, much to her displeasure. After dinner she challenged Adam to a game of chess, ready to get rid of some of her frustrations by slaughtering Adam at the game. She was a better chess player than almost anyone she'd ever played with.

But not better than Adam.

He had her check-mate in an amazingly short time. Losing to Adam did nothing for Roxanne's mood, although, like the good sport she was, she hid it well. Kate was secretly delighted. Roxanne needed a good thump on her arrogant little head now and then. She had little or no respect for the male of the species, but was seldom without a man. Her taste in men was rather eclectic and she'd had an impressive array ever since college, including a Nepalese prince (or at least he'd said he was a prince), an Australian opal digger and how Khalim with his belly dancers.

Kate found that she enjoyed being with Adam, that his conservative appearance hid an interesting personality. The magazine profile had depicted him as a talented and ambitious businessman, which no doubt he was, yet he did not present himself that way when he spoke about his work. There was another side to him and it intrigued her. Somewhere inside him was still hidden the small-town boy. From the few things he had told her about his childhood, she'd composed a mental image of him as a conscientious little boy whose life was organised around his schoolwork, his cow and his paper route; a boy who mowed the lawn for his neighbours and saved every penny for college.

He'd lost his father at the age of nine and there was no way his mother could ever afford to pay for a college education. He had ended up as a graduate of Harvard.

Despite his modest background, Adam seemed to feel perfectly at home in the sophisticated, worldly circles he moved in now. He was neither impressed nor intimidated by power and wealth. There was something very strong and solid at the core of him and she was drawn to it instinctively. It was something that had been absent in the other men she'd known, and she'd never realised it until now. *Substance*, she thought. *Adam has substance.*

Still, she could not help but tease him about his cow and his conservative ties and his love for mashed potatoes. He took her teasing without offence, kept wearing his ties as he had before and had his hair cut when it showed the first signs of not being really short any more.

'Why did you do that?' she asked. 'It looked nice a little longer! I could run my fingers through it. Now they just slide off.'

'First my ties, now my hair.' He looked at her with mock despair. 'And I keep hoping you'll look past the exterior and love me for myself.'

'Oh, shut up, Adam!'

Kate dressed up in a number of her more flamboyant outfits. She looked good, she knew—she had a flair for line and colour, but she couldn't imagine Adam not preferring his women a little more classically attired. Although, when she'd worn Samantha's dress, he had seen through her and known that for her it had merely been a costume. Apparently, he was accepting her the way she was, and she had to admit to a pang of guilt over her own criticisms of him. Why couldn't she just keep her big mouth shut?

Adam had promised to pick her up at seven on

Saturday night and she was ready when she heard his knock on the door. She wasn't ready for the sight that greeted her: Adam in casual clothes, hand in hand with a scruffy-looking little boy. His jeans were too short, his hair too long, his sneakers worn out.

'Hi,' she said brightly, hiding her surprise. 'Come in. I just need to get my bag.'

'Kate, this is Nicky. Nicky, this is Ms Flannigan.'

'Nice to meet you, Nicky.'

The boy said nothing. He stared at Kate with wide eyes. I must look pretty glamorous to him, Kate thought, amused by his admiring gaze.

'We've been to the zoo,' Adam stated, as if he regularly took scruffy little boys to the zoo. 'We were late and then the traffic was bad, and I decided I'd better just pick you up before I took him home.'

'Sure, no problem,' said Kate, reaching for her wrap and her clutch bag. 'Let's go.'

We must be a strange sight, Kate thought—me, dressed to kill, this shabby-looking little boy, and Adam in jeans and a sport shirt. She couldn't suppress a smile when she saw the curious look the doorman threw in their direction. She waved at him, and he arched his brows at her in question.

'What did you like most about the zoo?' Kate asked Nicky as they drove away in Adam's car.

There was a short pause. 'The monkeys,' he said at last. 'They're funny.' No fun showed in the serious little face. So this was Nicky, the boy Adam had taken out to see the dinosaurs last week, and to the zoo today. He was about five or six, she guessed. He had deep-blue eyes in a thin little face with a pointed chin. His ears were rather big and stood out a bit too much from his head. He was a homely child and her heart went out to him.

'Did you see any baboons?' she asked.

'I . . . I don't know.'

'They're mean and ugly. I was working in Africa one time and a baboon stole my hat. He snatched it right off my head and ran away with it.'

The blue eyes widened in surprise. 'Really? Were you in a real jungle?'

'It wasn't really a jungle—just woods. We were in a little bus with the top open and I was looking around through my binoculars. Suddenly, from the trees, a whole bunch of baboons jumped right on top of the roof. One snatched my hat. I ducked right away and we closed the roof and drove away. They stayed on the roof for a while before they jumped off. They made a terrible noise.'

'Were you scared?'

She grinned at him. 'Maybe a little bit. Baboons can hurt you. You have to be careful.'

He sighed. 'I wish I could go to Africa to see the monkeys.'

'Maybe you will, when you're grown up. What do you want to be when you're big?'

He shrugged. 'Maybe a policeman, or a soldier.'

Kate nodded. She was suddenly aware that Adam had not said a word. She also noticed that they were somewhere on the Lower East Side. She kept up the chatter with the boy until Adam drew up to a block of squalid apartments and stopped. He turned and smiled at the boy, ruffling his hair.

'Okay, young man, let's take you back to your mother.' He looked at Kate. 'Why don't you stay here? I'll be right back.'

'Fine.' She watched them enter the door, Adam's hand resting protectively on Nicky's shoulder. The street was a depressing place with its grey, cheerless buildings. Not a slum, quite, but certainly a poor neighbourhood. A battered car, divested of its wheels, crouched by the curb. A newspaper drifted across the street and an overflowing dustbin was being explored by a hungry dog. Children played touch football, their excited voices drifting towards her on the muggy air, reaching her ears through the closed windows.

It was only minutes before Adam appeared again.

'Sorry about that,' he said as he slid behind the wheel. 'Things did not quite go according to plan.'

She smiled. 'I have a lot of experience with things not going according to plan. As a matter of fact, I thrive on it.'

'I don't doubt it for a minute.' He started the engine and drove slowly out of the street.

'Not a very uplifting place, this,' she said casually.

'No.'

They were silent for a while, the subject of Nicky an intangible presence between them. If something wasn't wrong, why did he not say anything? She stared out the window. She didn't want to ask when it was so obvious he didn't want to talk about it. Traffic moved agonisingly slowly. As they waited for a red light, Adam glanced at his watch and frowned. 'I'm afraid we'll be late. The reservation is for eight and I need to go home and change first. I'll call and see if we can change it for nine.'

'Or we can go somewhere else.'

'But I promised to take you to this place. I'm truly sorry.'

She shrugged. 'We'll make it another time. I plan to live a long life.'

His smile warmed her. 'I'm glad you're so flexible.'

She grinned. 'Like a rubber band.' The way she lived she had to be.

She'd not been to his apartment before. It was on the top floor of a rather expensive-looking building, which did not surprise her. Once inside she looked around curiously, noticing to her surprise a baby grand piano at the other end of the room. A piano? Did Adam play the piano? She hadn't known that. Well, there were other things she didn't know about him.

'Make yourself comfortable,' Adam offered. 'I'll run through the shower. I won't be long. Can I pour you a drink first?'

'No thanks.' She picked up a newspaper. 'I'll read the comics.' She waved the paper. 'Go ahead.'

The comics only took a few minutes, and they didn't make her laugh. She got up and restlessly walked around the room. It was furnished comfortably and stylishly, but had somehow an empty look about it. There were no flowers or plants or throw pillows—no little homey touches. She slid her hands along the top of the piano. What else was there she didn't know about him? Who was this little boy?

Could it possibly be his son? She stood very still, staring down on the black and white keys. *Your imagination is working overtime*, she told herself. How could that scrawny little thing in those worn clothes possibly be his son? If Adam was paying for his support, he wouldn't be living in that depressing, grey street. Or maybe he would. What did she know about this man, anyway?

She knew a lot about him. That he liked mashed potatoes. That he enjoyed taking out a little boy to the zoo. That he didn't care for parties. That he'd beaten Roxanne at chess. That he hadn't tried to seduce her at the first possible opportunity . . .

'*I'm not exactly perfect myself, either.*' Adam's words echoed in her memory. Oh, damn, damn, she thought miserably. What am I getting myself into now? Maybe he lied to me. Maybe he was married once, or maybe

Nicky is a son by a woman he was never married to in the first place.

She didn't want to think he had lied to her. Not that he'd be the first one, but this time it mattered more. There had to be another explanation. Please, she prayed, let there be another explanation.

She studied the music. Mostly classic. Mozart, Debussy. She closed her eyes and she could almost hear the music rippling through the room. She visualised Adam behind the piano, his lean brown fingers dancing lightly over the keys. Suddenly she wanted nothing more than to hear Adam play, to be wrapped up in the magic of music and forget everything else.

A door opened and closed. Footsteps in the hall. Adam entered the room, tossing a teal-blue jacket on to a chair. 'We're in luck. I have a reservation for nine,' he announced, knotting his tie with blind expertise.

'Good,' she said cheerfully. 'I'm famished.' Her hands stroked the shiny wood of the piano. 'I didn't know you played the piano.'

'I never mentioned it?' He came towards her, shouldering into his jacket.

'No. Do you play often?'

'Every chance I get, which isn't so often with my schedule.'

'Would you play for me some time?'

'Any time you like.'

'Could we come back here later tonight?' she asked impulsively. 'After we've eaten?'

He looked into her eyes and she could feel herself grow warm, but she did not avert her gaze.

'I'd like that,' he said quietly. 'Sometimes I get very tired of always being out.'

'I know.'

They were standing close, not touching. She could feel the warmth of his body radiating on her bare arms. He reached out, running his hand through her hair.

'Kate . . .' he said softly, and it was almost a sigh.

Her heart began to race and then they moved together, slipping into each other's arms, fitting perfectly against each other. He kissed her deeply, hungrily, and she clung to him dizzily. It was happening again. Her heart was racing and a treacherous weakness was invading her limbs. She moved back a little, trying to keep her balance, and leaned into the piano keys. An ear-rending cacophony of sounds burst into the silence, and she jumped away from the piano.

For a moment they stared at each other before they broke into laughter.

'You did that on purpose,' he accused.

She shook her head, still laughing. 'No. I did not! Why would I?'

'Oh, I think you know why.' He took her hand. 'We'd better go, or we won't make our nine o'clock reservation, either.'

Kate was bright and funny that evening, entertaining him with her stories of her adventures, but all the time she could feel something gnawing inside her. Against all her intentions and inclinations, she was falling for this man, and she wasn't sure she trusted him. She was sorry now that she'd asked to come back to his apartment after dinner. Was there any way she could gracefully get out of it? She couldn't think of anything. She couldn't even plead a headache. Only yesterday she'd told him she seldom had one. She covered up her unease with bright chatter as they drove back to his apartment. Apparently he was not deceived.

'I have the uncanny feeling that something is wrong,' he said as soon as they were inside. 'Let's have it, all right?' He gently pushed her down on the soft couch, lowering himself next to her.

'What makes you think something is wrong?'

'You were just a bit too bright and too funny. So, what is it?'

Kate took a deep breath. 'I've been wondering about Nicky and why you won't talk about him.'

'It's not a happy story,' he said quietly. The shadows were there again in his eyes.

'Is he your son?'

'What if he were, Kate?'

She sighed. 'Oh, Adam, knowing you had a son would hardly be a shock! Many men your age have kids. But . . . it would mean you'd been lying to me. And I . . . I don't think I'd trust you any more.'

He took her hand. 'I never lied to you, Kate. Nicky isn't my son. He's a little boy I take out on weekends when I'm in town.' He looked down on his hand holding hers. 'He has no father to do that. His father is dead. And I . . .' He paused, looking up and holding her gaze. 'I feel . . . responsible for his death.'

CHAPTER FOUR

ADAM came to his feet, turning his back on her. 'It happened last December,' he said tonelessly. 'I was driving home one night. There were icy patches on the road. Nicky's father was passing me in the other lane. He hit one of the icy spots, went into a tail spin and ended up in front of my car. I hit him. He was thrown out of his car.'

'But Adam, I don't see how that makes *you* responsible.'

He turned and faced her. 'Oh, I'm not responsible in the eyes of the law. I didn't have a drop of alcohol in me. I wasn't speeding. I wasn't driving recklessly in any way. I didn't cause the accident.' He paused. 'But I could have avoided it.' He sighed heavily. 'You know, Kate, I was in no shape to drive. I'd come home on a straight flight from Tokyo the night before. I had four hours of sleep, got up, had a cup of coffee and went to the office. I had so much work to do, I was too busy to have lunch. I grabbed a leftover doughnut. I worked overtime. I quit at seven and drove home to fix myself some dinner and go to bed.' He paused for a moment. 'I had not eaten all day. I hadn't had more than a few hours of sleep in the last few days. I was a goddamned zombie. If my reactions had been a bit swifter, I would have avoided hitting that car and Nicky would still have a father. It was irresponsible to drive that night but I never gave it a thought. The law does not specify that you must be reasonably rested and have food in your stomach to drive a car.'

'How can you possibly know for sure that you wouldn't have hit that car had you been in better shape? These things happen so fast, there's no time to do anything!'

He pushed his hands in his pockets. 'Kate, I am a very good driver. I've never had as much as a fender-bender and I've been on the road in more countries than New York has rats. I've driven on the right side of the road, on the left side of the road, I've driven in Rome, Jakarta, São Paulo. You can't begin to count the maniacs I have encountered and the accidents I have avoided. I *know* I could have avoided this one if only I'd had my wits about me. I would have reacted faster, I know that.'

'But the man was speeding and he was the one to hit the icy spot! *He* was the one who drove irresponsibly and recklessly!'

He gave her a wry smile. 'Don't try to convince me I shouldn't feel the way I do. It's been tried before. I feel guilty about the whole sorry affair and I suppose I always will.'

'And Nicky's mother? Does she blame you?'

He gave a humourless laugh. 'No, not even she does. I went to see her after the accident. I asked her if there was anything I could do, anything she needed, but she refused. She's a proud woman and wanted nothing from me. "I don't want your charity or your guilt," she said to me. I was not at fault, she told me. Her husband had recently lost his job and had been drinking heavily. He'd not been drinking before the accident, but he was speeding. The only thing she'll let me do is take Nicky out sometimes—to the zoo, or to play ball in the park or whatever.' He paused for a moment. 'A couple of months after the accident, one Saturday when I picked up Nicky, I realised she was pregnant. She hadn't told me. She might not even have been sure herself at the time of the accident. It was like a blow in the stomach.' He shook his head. 'I can't begin to tell you what I felt.'

Kate got up and came towards him. She put her arms around him, resting her head on his shoulder. For endless minutes they just stood like that. She didn't know what to say. It was so much like Adam to deal with that tragedy in this way, to feel responsible for something no one else held him accountable for. Conservative Adam with his high standards and expectations of himself.

'Why don't you play the piano for me now?' she asked softly.

It was the music that chased away the spell of sadness. Adam was a wonderful player and for almost an hour he transported her with his music. Curled up in a chair she watched him play, saw the total absorption on his face. She felt warm excitement as she listened. This was not mere virtuosity, technique. The sounds drifting around her were infused with something more profound than mere skill, something that came from deep inside him—a joy, a tenderness of the soul. There were depths to Adam she would enjoy discovering.

Finally he turned to her and smiled.

'Enough?'

It wasn't easy coming back to reality and she sighed with the effort. She shook her head. 'Never enough. That was truly wonderful, Adam. I don't remember ever having enjoyed music so much.'

His eyes lit up with pleasure. 'I'm glad. Would you like a glass of wine?'

'That would be nice. And before I forget, could I borrow that book you mentioned yesterday?'

'*The Spiral Road?* Sure. Come on, I'll get it.'

She followed him into his study, a carpeted room

with a large desk and walls full of books. Several framed pictures hung on one wall and when she drew closer to look, she noticed one of a cow, with a blue ribbon on its halter. She laughed, and Adam turned to look at her.

'Minnie, the sacred cow,' she said, mocking him.

'Don't go criticising my cow. There's only so much beating my ego can take. Here's your book.'

'Your ego is in no danger whatsoever.' She reached out to take the book from him, and he took the opportunity to grab her wrist and draw her against him.

She resisted. 'It's time for me to go home.'

'No, it isn't. Not before I kiss you.' He bent closer, touching his lips to her left temple.

She squirmed away. 'I don't want to be kissed tonight.'

'That's too bad. You'll just have to suffer through it, just like the last few nights.'

The last few nights. Heaven help her if he kissed her the way he had kissed her the last few nights. 'You were having fun with me, weren't you? Playing games with me. Well, now it's my turn.' She smiled sweetly. 'No kissing. I'm going home.'

He was running his tongue around the edge of her ear. 'You made one big mistake,' he whispered. 'I've got you captive, right here in my den.'

'You're an animal, Adam.' She pushed half-heartedly at his chest, feeling the treacherous thrills of excitement beginning to capture her senses.

'Aren't you lucky.'

'Hah! The conceit! Let go of me!'

'You'd be so disappointed if I did.' He unzipped her dress and put his hands flat against her bare back. 'Don't fight it,' he whispered in her ear. 'It's a lost cause, you know.'

The dress begin to slip off her shoulders. 'Stop it.' she said fiercely.

'I can't. You think it was easy leaving you every time I brought you home this past week?'

'I'm glad to hear you suffered. Serves you right for doing what you did.'

He blew softly into her ear. 'What did I do?'

She twisted her face away and the dress fell all the way off her shoulders. 'You *know* what you did!' She tried to push the dress back up, but he was holding her so she couldn't reach.

He laughed softly. 'You deserved it.' His hands unhooked her bra and slipped the straps off her shoulders. 'You have the arrogance to think you can bend fate to your own desires.'

'Meaning that *my* fate is whatever *you* desire, is that it?' It was not easy staying calm. She trembled with his nearness, the feel of his hands on her back.

He smiled into her eyes. 'Sounds good, but that's not what I mean. Fate is whatever there is between us that you are so very busy denying.' One finger gently touched her left nipple and a quiver of desire rippled through her. She closed her eyes.

'Lust. You call that fate?'

'It's more than lust, Kate.'

It was impossible to work up the energy for a fight. Her heart wasn't in it. Her heart was too busy with something altogether different. 'Like what?' she whispered.

He brushed his lips across hers. 'Something special, something wonderful. You made me discover a part of me I didn't know existed. You make me feel . . . alive. It feels so good to be with you.'

Yes, she thought, but her mouth did not utter the words and the silence seemed to stretch. The game was over. There was no use in fighting her own feelings, to deny what was the truth: that it would be impossible to get him out of her life. She longed for him with a deep, painful ache, and she knew he could see it in her eyes. She looked away, but he took her chin and forced her to look at him.

'I'll take you home, if you want me to.'

Her throat went dry. 'No,' she said huskily.

He kissed her deeply, held her tightly against him and sweet warmth flooded her. She pressed closer, her breasts crushing against his chest.

He released her suddenly, sweeping her up into his arms and carried her out of the study into his bedroom. They fell on to the bed together, clinging to each other, not letting go, kissing, touching until she felt nothing but the need and the urgency like fire in her blood.

He slid the dress down her hips, her legs, kissing her stomach, her thighs, as he moved it along. He took her panties off in the same fashion and the sensuous feel of his lips as they trailed a path down her body built up an unbearable tension.

He rolled off the bed to take off his clothes and she watched him as he quickly stripped off his shirt, aware of his eyes as they surveyed her body stretched out naked on the bed. For a fleeting moment she felt uneasy at his silent scrutiny, feeling exposed and vulnerable, but the feeling passed as she saw the look in his eyes.

'You're beautiful,' he whispered and the breath caught in her throat. No one had ever looked at her with such a heady mixture of desire and tenderness and love. She wished there was something she could say to him, yet she knew no words to make him understand.

His chest was covered with dark, curly hair, disappearing behind the waistband of his slacks. He

unbuckled the belt and unzipped his slacks. He wore
dark blue pants and once they were gone too, the sight
of his naked body took her breath away—all beautiful,
muscular sleekness. Flat stomach, slim hips, long
strong legs—smooth, clean lines, utterly male. And he
wanted her.

Her stomach tightened and her heart began to race.
She wanted to get up and touch him, curl her fingers
into the hair on his chest, run her hand down the
plane of his stomach, press herself against him and feel
the heat of his body. She could not tear her eyes away
from him. Her cheeks flushed as his eyes met hers. His
lips curled in a faint smile. 'There isn't any way to be
subtle about this,' he said as he slid next to her in bed.
He wrapped his arms around her, holding her close,
and she felt a shudder go through him. 'I want you
very, very much.'

The feel of his body against her was pure sensuous
pleasure. 'I want you too,' she whispered. 'No more
games.'

'No more games.'

She fought a moment of panic. After tonight
nothing would be the same again. Adam wasn't a man
for one night only. And where it would lead to, she
didn't know. Yet she couldn't resist the irresistible.
And when the regret came, and the tears and the pain,
she would know they were the price she had to pay.
Maybe this time it won't happen, she thought. *Maybe
this time it will be different.*

Fleeting fear, fleeting thoughts. Adam's mouth and
his deep, sensuous kiss obliterated it all. She yielded to
him, answering his kiss, exploring his body with her
hands, touching, marvelling at the feel of it. Stroking,
kissing, discovering, a wonderful mutual delight in the
intimacy of the big bed.

Only the glow of one small lamp illuminated the

room. His shadowed face with the shifting expressions of tenderness and passion was the most beautiful face she'd ever seen. I love him, she thought, and it was a simple truth as they lay together in the rosy light, but one that made her heady with its power and dizzy with fear. *Don't think! Don't think!* she said silently.

Adam's mouth rested against her breast. 'Kate,' he said softly, 'I've never felt about anybody, the way I feel about you. I've never felt more alive and whole than I've felt this past week with you.' He raised his head slightly. 'Do you believe me?'

'Yes,' she whispered.

But a week was only a week, or was it eight days? Yet it seemed she'd known him so much longer than that. So much had been crammed in those evenings together. Time was precious as gold—every hour, every minute counted. Tomorrow she'd be on a plane again . . . *Don't think! Don't think!*

'I wish I had words to tell you how I feel,' he said, echoing her own thoughts. He smiled down at her, running his fingers softly along the outline of her mouth.

Her throat went dry. 'I don't need words,' she whispered. 'Just . . . kiss me, hold me . . . it feels so good, so good . . .'

His mouth was warm on her breast, sending electric shivers of delight quivering through her. He slid his body up over hers, touching her with every inch of him. His breathing was ragged and she sensed his growing urgency. She felt the heavy thump of his heart against her breast and her senses went soaring.

'Adam . . .' she whispered. She heard him draw in his breath. She pressed herself closer to him, inviting him to come to her and he shifted his body, fitting it to hers. There was nothing but exquisite sensation, a spiralling of feverish passion, an absence of time and space until all tension broke in mutual spasms of glorious, wondrous release.

When sanity returned she lay in the circle of his arms, breathless and sated. She hadn't known it could be this good, this loving and wonderfully satisfying. Her cheek rested against his chest, the hair tickling her nose. The fingers of one of his hands were playing with her curls, the other hand covered her breast, warm, intimate.

'Some lover you are,' she whispered, kissing his chest.

'Mmm . . . and you.'

She was glad he didn't give a flip answer. She sighed, snuggling closer, drowsy with content. His hand was on the nape of her neck, his mouth in her hair.

'You smell so good,' he said softly. 'And you feel so warm and soft.' His hand stroked her thigh. 'You belong in my bed, Kate. All this week I kept looking at you, wondering what it would feel like to hold you in my arms, to touch your breasts, to make love to you. You've got the sexiest mouth I've ever seen, you nearly drove me wild.'

'Don't stop now; go on.' She touched her tongue to his chest, tickling him.

'It's your turn.'

'All right. You taste good and I loved the way you made love to me. And I wondered all week if you'd wear boxer shorts, and if you did, I couldn't possibly go to bed with you. I just didn't know how to ask you.'

He shook with laughter. 'Why couldn't you go to bed with me if I wore boxer shorts?'

'They'd look funny on you and I'd have to laugh and it would spoil the mood.'

'That would have been very serious. Think of what

you would have missed, and only because of some prejudice about boxer shorts.'

'Men who make love like you don't wear boxer shorts.'

'You told me your theory about men wearing ties. You have one about men wearing boxer shorts?'

She grinned. 'Yes, I do. You want to hear it?'

'No.'

That was just as well. She would have had to do some fast thinking to come up with something, and she wasn't up to that just now.

'What part of yourself did I make you discover?' she asked.

'The fun, happy, light-hearted part. You make me laugh.'

'You never laughed before you met me?'

He grinned. 'Only if I really had to.'

'You poor, deprived man. Why was that?'

'Life always seemed so serious. My mother was a real worrier. There never was much money.' He shrugged. 'Maybe it was against my basic nature. I always had big things on my mind—college, making a career, seeing the world. There never seemed much time for fun.'

'Now you've done everything—college, Harvard no less; you have a career and you've seen all the garden sports of the world. Now it's time for fun.' She moved her face level with his. 'Kiss me, please?'

He cradled her face, kissing her with so much sweet tenderness, her heart swelled with love. So different now than the passion of a short while ago, yet so utterly delightful in its own way. When he drew back, his eyes were full of love as he looked into hers. Then he smiled, drawing her head down on his shoulder.

'Let me hold you while you sleep,' he said.

*   *   *

Sunlight tickled her eyes when she awoke and as soon as she opened them she closed them again and turned over, pushing her face into the pillow. She didn't want to wake up. This was a comfortable bed. Her body felt heavy with sleep and was not at all eager to move. Her mind was still fuzzy. She tried to concentrate.

Where was she? She looked around. This was not a hotel room. It was Adam's room. She was in Adam's bed.

Where was Adam?

She was wide awake now. She almost fell out of bed in her haste, rushed into the bathroom and splashed water over her face. On a hook behind the door hung a short, terry bathrobe. She pulled it on. Not short on her. Came halfway down her calves. Oh well, never mind. It smelled good. Like Adam.

She found him in the living-room, drinking coffee and reading the Sunday paper. He looked up when she approached him and a grin spread across his face.

'Not your colour,' he said.

'What? This? No, it sure isn't.' Dark blue made her look washed out.

'Come here.' He reached out his hand and she came to him. He drew her on to his lap, covering her mouth and kissing her deeply. His hands slid inside the robe.

'Let's go back to bed,' he whispered.

'I can't.' She drew back, breathless. 'I've got to go. My plane leaves in three hours and I haven't even packed yet.'

He grew very still. 'Right,' he said after a moment. 'Morocco. The barbarians.' He kissed her hard, then slid her off his knees. 'Get ready. I'll fix you some breakfast.'

He took her home, stayed with her while she packed and drove her to Kennedy Airport. She wished she could have just taken a taxi. She was beginning to feel more and more depressed as they waited for her to board. In four weeks she'd be back in New York. By then Adam would be in Australia.

'I'll call you,' he said, kissing her for the last time.

She wondered when. And from where.

The first she heard from him was not via the telephone but through a card she found in her post. On it was pictured a giant artificial pineapple with tiny people entering a door at the bottom and others standing on top of it in the shade of its palm-like green crown. According to the back of the card, this amazing structure was a tourist attraction in Queensland in the tropical north of Australia, housing an observation desk and audio-visual displays of pineapple production.

And they say Americans have no taste, Adam had scrawled on the back. *Wish you were here so we could explore this marvel of twentieth century architecture together.*

The promised phone call arrived one night as she was sitting on a quiet verandah in Kashmir enjoying the cooing of the mynah birds and the fragrances of pines and chinar trees. A manservant with coal-black hair and a pristine white suit told her of the phone call in impeccable Indian English. She rushed up the stairs to take the call in her room. Breathlessly she picked up the receiver.

'Adam!' It was all she could manage, but the pleasure in her voice was hard to hide—not that that was particularly necessary, but cool and sophisticated it was not.

'How are you?'

She took a deep breath. 'I'm fine. Replete with *dum murghi Kashmir.*'

'Sounds dangerous.'

'It's only chicken. With fifteen different spices, give or take a few.'

'And how were the Berbers this time?'

'The Berbers were fine, too. I even got a proposal of marriage.'

'Since you're in Kashmir now, you obviously didn't accept.'

'Oh, but it was tempting, Adam! He had very sexy eyes, wild, mysterious. Very promising. Of course that was all I could see.' She sighed regretfully.

'But you broke his heart.'

'His liver, Adam, his liver.'

Adam groaned. 'Forgive me.'

'He was pretty persistent, though. Seemed to think we should try it for a year. If he hadn't convinced me by then that he was the perfect husband, we could get a divorce.'

'One, two, three.'

'Actually, yes. Quite easy and not uncommon. Women do a certain amount of husband hopping there. Not altogether bad, you know. If a man wants to keep his wife, he'd better treat her right or she's gone in a flash. Remind me next time to tell you about it.'

'When I'm with you, I don't want to talk about the Berbers, Kate.'

'No? What do you want to talk about?'

'Let's not discuss it over the phone. It's very distressing with all those thousands of miles and one and half oceans between us.'

Kate laughed. 'I don't even know where you are.'

'On an island in the Caribbean. Not bad.'

'I'm sure not. Lots of gorgeous women, I bet.'

'A few,' he agreed.

'So why do you call me? The oceans, the miles . . .'

'None of the beauties here have red hair.'

'Neither have I.'

'What?'

'I don't have red hair. Not any more. I dyed it black.'

There was a lengthy pause. Static crackled along the line in the silence. 'You didn't,' he said with quiet menace.

'I did. Cut it too, real short. Looks cute.'

'*Cute*?' He was almost shouting, which Kate found very satisfying. She grinned into the mouthpiece.

'You'll like it, Adam. And it's so much easier, you know. It dries faster and it looks neat and . . .'

'*Cute*?' he repeated, as if it were a dirty word. 'Kate! You are not *cute*! Sexy, gorgeous, seductive, infuriating, yes, but *not cute*!'

'Thank you.' She was beginning to enjoy this conversation.

'Why did you do it?' He sounded wounded.

'I wanted a change. I wanted to get rid of all that red. It stands out too much.'

'I *like* outstanding women,' he protested, the misuse of the word no doubt intentional.

'Well, that's good, Adam. I'm still very much the same outstanding woman. And you'll like my hair, don't worry. I had it done in Paris, by André himself.' She knew she'd made a mistake as soon as the words were out. She hadn't been near Paris in months, and Adam knew her schedule.

'Kate! You're lying to me!'

She laughed. 'Scared you, didn't I? Shame on you. I thought you liked *me*, not my hair.'

'I like everything, *including* the wrapping.' He sighed. 'That was a dirty trick. Not nice, Kate, not nice.'

'Whatever gave you the idea that I'm nice?'

'Mmm, come to think of it, I don't know.'

'Listen, did you call me just to insult me?'

'Actually, no. I have a question for you.'

Kate crossed her legs, She was sitting on the bed, on top of the cotton bedspread with its multi-coloured Indian design. 'Okay, shoot.'

'How's your French?'

'*Comme ci, comme ça.* But I have news for you. They don't speak French in Kashmir.'

'They do in the south of France.'

'True.'

'How would you like to spend some time in a secluded villa on the Côte d'Azur?'

'Busy busy at this time of the year. *Tout le monde* hangs out there, you know. Besides, what am I going to do in a secluded villa all by myself?'

'I was thinking of joining you there to entertain you. And we don't have to mingle with the masses too much. Maybe an occasional dash into the market to stock up on food. For the rest I think we don't need to spend much time away from the house.'

Kate shifted the receiver to her other ear. 'Sounds like a very sinful proposition to me.'

'I hope so.'

'There is, of course, a small matter of timing. When did you want this little escapade to take place?'

'You told me you have a week's vacation planned for the end of this month.'

'So I do.'

'As it happens, I have, too.'

'Gee, whiz, such coincidence!'

'Isn't it? And I was looking through my little black book and it seemed the only one available is you.'

'Lucky me.'

There was a pause. 'No—lucky me.'

'Lucky us.'

'So you'll come?'

'Yes.'

The villa was not just any old house. It was a jewel of creative design, nestled in the cliffs as if it belonged there, part of the landscape, built to conform to the contours of the rocks. It was vast and cool, with large terraces, a wine cellar, a modern kitchen, a very private, walled-in garden with luxuriantly growing plants and trees, and a large teardrop swimming pool. Every day, Adam told her, a maid came in for a couple of hours to keep the place in order.

'Whose house is this?' Kate asked as they made their tour of the place. Beautiful carpets adorned the tiled floors. Comfortable furniture, upholstered in white, invited long and lazy lounging.

'It belongs to a friend of mine, an eccentric old millionaire of seventy-nine by the name of George McCoy. It's quite a story how I met him. I'll tell you some time.'

The master bedroom was large and light, with french doors opening on to its own terrace with white cane furniture and huge potted hydrangeas. Pink flowering creepers clung to the railings and in the distance the Mediterranean glittered seductively under the mid-morning sun. Inside, soft white carpeting and pale jade-green curtains and bedding created a cool yet intimate atmosphere.

'Not bad,' Kate decided. 'Why is your friend not here?'

'He's on a canoe trip down one of the Amazon tributaries.'

'Not alone, I hope.'

Adam grinned. 'I wouldn't be surprised. He's an old English colonial who lived for twenty-odd years in Borneo. He used to trek through the jungles with a medical team to save stone-age tribes from cholera epidemics. The stories he tells about that make your hair stand on end. Don't worry, old George can take care of himself.'

'Sounds like a fascinating character.'

'He is. Made his fortune in geraniums.'

'*Geraniums?*'

Adam laughed. 'Geranium oil, I should say. It's used in the perfume industry. Maybe you'll get a chance to meet good old George and you can ask him about it. He said he might be back by the end of the month. Then again, he may be gone for another three weeks.' He shrugged. 'Who knows?'

He pushed his hands into his pockets and surveyed the room. Then his eyes sought hers.

'Do you prefer a room of your own or would you like to share this one?'

The question took her aback a little. 'My, we are direct, aren't we?'

He gave a half-smile. 'I've found that directness often helps to avoid misunderstandings and confusion. In the West, that is,' he amended, his smile broadening. 'In business dealings in the East and in Africa, of course, it is often more beneficial to take roundabout ways—talk about the crops, the grand-children first. Do you want to talk about grand-children?'

'Oh, shut up, Adam! And I am not a business proposition! I am not going to answer this question! You take all the romance out of it! Businessmen!' She stomped out of the room.

He had met her at Nice airport amid a maddening crowd of tourists milling around like a confused batch of army ants. Her heart had leaped with excitement when she'd finally spotted him, and his smile, when he saw her, had made her tingle from top to toe. It had been six weeks since she'd last seen him and the attraction had not faded. She'd hoped, perversely, that it would have. Life would be a lot easier without a man like Adam on her mind.

He wound his way towards her. 'Hello, Kate.'

'Hi,' she said lightly, giving him a wide smile. She wanted to throw herself into his arms, but he did not invite it, nor did he touch or kiss her. Much too conservative for public displays of affection, she told herself as she looked into his eyes. Affection? she questioned silently. Affection, is that it? Hey, don't kid yourself. Look at his eyes. We're talking major passion here.

It wasn't a long drive to the villa and here she was standing on this beautiful shady terrace digesting his businesslike question of whether she wanted a room of her own or to share the big one with him. Well, she'd decided what to do. She turned and walked back inside and began to examine the other bedrooms. There were three more, all ready for occupation, by the looks of them. In the hall she found her suitcase, noticing Adam's was gone, and took it to the bedroom furthest away from the big one. Let him figure this out.

She tossed the suitcase on the bed and opened it, noticing the flat, wrapped package on top. The present for Adam. A framed picture of her in full Berber regalia, taken in Morocco. She took it out carefully and put it in a dresser drawer.

She'd barely started unpacking when Adam appeared in the doorway, wearing nothing more than black swimming trunks and a white towel draped around his neck. The sight of his deeply tanned torso, so nearly naked, made her heart begin to gallop and her blood race wildly through her veins. He lounged against the doorpost, giving her a mocking smile.

'Here you are.' He surveyed the suitcase on the bed. 'So you've decided.'

She controlled herself with an effort, producing a sunny smile. 'I like this room—nice colour scheme.'

'Playing hard to get?'

She fixed him with a stony stare. 'I'm not playing!'

'Neither am I.' He advanced into the room, stopping in front of her with only inches to spare. He put his hands on her head, stroking the curls. He looked into her eyes, then slowly lowered his gaze to her mouth.

Her senses quickened alarmingly. Standing as still as possible, she tried not to show her reactions. There was no way to move—the edge of the bed was pushing into her thighs. She didn't want to move, at least not away. She wanted to put her hands on his chest, yet with a strength she didn't know she possessed, she let her arms hang limply by her side.

With one thumb he traced the line of her jaw. She closed her eyes and took an unsteady breath. He was so close, she could feel the warmth of his body. His breath fanned her cheek and the scent of aftershave was in her nose. Her body tingled with his nearness, her senses remembering that last night they'd been together in New York. She ran her tongue over her lips, feeling her knees grow weak.

He didn't kiss her and she ached with longing for the feel and taste of his mouth. Opening her eyes she looked right into his. They were dark and intense and her heart leaped. For endless minutes they stared at each other, not moving any closer, the silence alive with electricity around them.

'You're not playing fair,' she whispered at last.

'Neither are you.' His hands dropped away from her and he took a step backward. 'I'll see you by the pool when you've finished unpacking. I'm going for a swim.' Before she could say a word, he strode out of the room and she stared after him in stupefaction. His control was truly phenomenal. Her knees gave way and she sat down on the edge of the bed, heaving a deep sigh.

She was trembling. 'Idiot,' she muttered to herself. 'Don't go ruining everything. A week is all you've got.'

In mere minutes she changed into a bright yellow bikini and rushed out to the pool. Adam was swimming around in circles, his muscled arms cleaving through the water in powerful strokes, trailing glistening drops of water through the air. It was a beautiful sight—a picture of strength and vitality and grace. For several minutes she stood at the edge of the pool, watching him, her blood singing.

When he'd passed her once again, she dived into the water and surfaced in the middle of the pool, shaking her curls like a poodle. He noticed her then and was next to her with a couple of swift strokes.

'That was fast,' he said, eyebrows lifted in surprise.

'I didn't unpack. I thought I'd have a swim first.'

He reached out and put his hands on her waist, pulling her to him. She put her arms around his neck and stopped treading water, looking into his face. Water was dripping from his hair down his forehead. His eyes looked into hers, a faint smile curving his mouth.

'You don't want to fight any more?' he enquired.

'If you stop being the practical businessman. They don't allow businessmen in Paradise, didn't you know?'

'I was only trying to make it less awkward. I didn't want you to think I automatically assumed you'd want to share my bed.' He grinned. 'I was hoping, of course.'

'Of course,' she mimicked. 'You're such a gentleman, Adam. Anyway, there are other ways to find out, you know. Romance . . . seduction . . .'

There was a devilish glint in his eyes. 'I thought modern career women didn't want romance and seduction.'

'You have a lot to learn, Adam Cooper.' Swiftly she disentangled herself from his grasp and swam away as fast as she could.

It was not much of a chase. He had caught her in mere minutes and she clung to him breathlessly.

He laughed softly. 'All right. Romance and seduction it is.' With his legs and one hand he moved them away from the middle of the pool to the shallow area and anchored his feet to the bottom. Hands on her hips, he pressed her to him, capturing her mouth and kissing her deeply, his tongue finding hers in an intimate caress.

Wild longing leaped through her body. She would surely have drowned had he not held her to him. Strength flowed out of her. She felt liquid, weightless, part of the water, yet warmer, much warmer. One of his hands moved up and unhooked her bikini top, then loosened the tie around her neck. The water lapped softly against her bare breasts as the scrap of yellow material floated away.

'Would you like to explore the wine cellar?' he whispered in her ear.

'What for?'

'To find a nice bottle of champagne.'

'No.'

'Champagne is romantic. Don't you like it?'

'I do, but I'd rather . . .'

His mouth covered hers, silencing her. After endless breathless moments, he drew back, lifted her into his arms, and carried her out of the water and indoors.

CHAPTER FIVE

In the bathroom he set her on her feet again, taking a towel from the rack and wrapping her in it. With another towel he began to dry her hair. She stood still, luxuriating in his ministrations, her eyes on his face. How long since she had last touched his face, kissed his mouth? She'd seen him in her dreams, but nothing could compare to the reality of being close to him. Drops of water clung to the hair on his chest. Desire curled inside her, a small, delicious flame promising fire. He was taking his time, then suddenly flung the towel aside, took the other one from around her body and began to dry himself with it.

His eyes swept over her body, lingering on her breasts, and the hungering in his gaze made her throat go dry.

'It's been a long time,' he said softly.

She swallowed. 'Yes.'

With casual swiftness he stripped off his swimming trunks and hung them on the rack, then wrapped his arms round her, drawing her against him. His body felt cool and damp, and a drop of water fell from his hair on to her cheek. She closed her eyes, searching to meet his mouth, and heat swept through her blood as his lips touched hers. It was a kiss full of fire, of longing—a kiss betraying the long lonely nights and the yearning for each other.

He moved down her body, kissing her breasts, her stomach. His hand slid down her hips and thighs, discarding the bikini bottom, and pressing his face against her belly in a convulsive embrace.

She felt light-headed and weak with longing, leaning against the cold tiled wall, heart pounding. He straightened, taking her arm and led her into the bedroom, drawing back the covers before pulling her down with him on the bed.

They made love with furious frenzy, which left them exhausted, yet dizzy with delight. For endless minutes he held her tightly, as if afraid she would vanish if he relaxed his hold.

'Oh, Kate,' he groaned. 'You don't know what you do to me.'

She laughed softly. 'Oh, but I do, Adam.'

He let out a ragged breath, raising his head to look into her eyes. 'I don't know if this makes sense, but I love you, Kate.'

Her heart lurched. 'I love you, too.' Saying the words was like taking a giant leap off a cliff, and she was falling . . . falling, not knowing if she had wings to fly. The terror was there, along with the delirious sense of freedom, for now she was no longer fighting reason. She nestled closer into the curve of his big, warm body, pressing her face against his shoulder. It felt safe and secure in his embrace. It felt like home.

'It doesn't have to make sense, you know,' she said. 'Maybe love never does.'

Kate gave him the Berber picture later that day and he looked at it for some time, a smile creeping around his mouth.

'And this exotic creature is really you?'

She nodded. 'Really, truly.' She glanced at the picture. A dark headdress covered her hair, forehead and mouth. It was decorated with strands of multi-coloured yarn from which dangled innumerable silvery coins. Her eyes were thickly outlined with kohl, a blotch of carmine coloured her cheeks and a dotted design adorned her nose. She'd taken on the demure look of a modest Berber maiden and the picture was hauntingly beautiful.

'A Berber girl with blue eyes.'

'They come in all colours. Blue-eyed blondes and green-eyed redheads, too. A legacy of European Vandals way back when.'

'The only way I can tell it's you is by that small beauty mark by your left eye. You love this, don't you? Dressing up.' There were sparks of humour in his eyes. 'First the virginal spinster, now this.'

Kate grinned. 'Yep. As a girl I used to play elaborate dress-up-games. I loved to pretend I was a queen or a jungle explorer, all kinds of things. My favourite one was a gypsy. I had a great costume for that one.'

'Not as great as this one.' Carefully he put the picture down and leaned over to kiss her. 'Thank you. It's very beautiful.'

'I thought it would look nice hanging next to Minnie.'

He threw back his head and laughed, then drew her into his arms and hugged her. 'Kate,' he whispered in her ear. 'You do my soul good.'

Kate's soul wasn't suffering either. The days were glorious—full of sunshine, laughter, delicious food and wine. Days of love, of romance and seduction. They explored the area—strolled through the narrow cobbled streets of ancient walled villages, visited Roman ruins, and browsed through the farmer's markets where fresh fish, all kinds of cheeses and newly baked bread were sold amid a mouthwatering variety of fruit, vegetables and herbs.

One morning they rented a boat and went sailing for the day, and one night they sat in a grassy field amid a number of other tourists and listened to an impromptu jazz concert. They had breakfast on the bedroom terrace, or went for croissants and coffee at a sidewalk café in the village. Kate enjoyed cooking and experimented with the purchases from the market. Other times they ate at one of the small restaurants or picturesque inns that abounded in the area. Every day they swam in the teardrop pool and made love in the jade-green room. Kate couldn't remember ever feeling happier.

A week is not enough, she kept thinking. *Not enough, not enough.*

'I have an idea,' she said late one afternoon. They were sitting by the pool, eating peaches.

'Am I going to like it?'

She wiped peach juice off her chin. 'You should.'

He leaned back in his lounger and stretched out his legs. 'Mmm . . . let's hear it.'

'I think the Crown Hotel Corporation should branch out into something different. Different types of resorts.'

'Such as what?'

'Well, I was thinking. I'd like to see them build villages in secluded places, build the houses with local materials in the local style. Keep everything simple, even the food. Give people an idea of what it's really like to live in a small tropical village. They'd learn how to make clay pots, weave blankets, carve out canoes, hunt, fish, whatever the local people do.' She began to elaborate on the idea, warming to the subject as her imagination sprouted new ideas.

He shook his head, breaking off her enthusiastic account in mid-sentence. 'CHC wouldn't be interested.'

She looked at him indignantly. 'Why not?'

'It's not what the CHC does. They're in the modern resort hotel business.'

'With bars and swimming pools and golf courses and tennis courts,' she said with contempt.

He shrugged, unperturbed. 'That's what the tourists want.' He selected another one of the luscious peaches from the bowl on the table between them and bit into it.

'Maybe because that's all they're offered!' She felt belligerent, ready for a fight. It did nothing for her rational thinking, she knew that, too.

'Not true. There's your agency.'

'And we're doing very well!'

'So are we.' He grinned at her. 'Our type of tourists don't want to sweat out their precious two weeks' vacation in a primitive tropical village. They want to be pampered and coddled. Not everybody is a Dr Livingstone.' He gave her a disarming smile. 'There's room for all of us out there, Kate.'

He was right, of course. She was just prejudiced and she knew it. She heaved a sigh and licked her lips. 'Anyway, why I dreamed up that idea was because we could do it together. You could do what you always do—the studying and researching. Then once it was all built, you could run it and study it for duplication, and I could deal with the visitors.'

'It wouldn't work, Kate.'

'Why not?'

'It sounds like an experiment, not a business enterprise. You'll never get anybody to finance it. It won't be cost-effective. There's no money in it.'

'How do you know that?' She felt on the defensive and she didn't like it.

'An educated guess. It *is* my business, you know. By nature these villages have to be small, which is one major factor. Also, the market for this sort of vacationing is very limited. Big business wants to do big business.'

Kate stared gloomily at the peach in her hand. There was a rotten spot on it. She shrugged. 'It was just an idea. I thought it would be nice to work together.' She forced herself to smile. 'Oh, well,' she added on a cheerful note, 'come to think of it, we'd probably get bored with each other in no time at all.'

He nodded solemnly, but his eyes were laughing. 'Probably.'

When the last day came, depression settled over her like a grey cloud. She was packing her suitcase late that afternoon when Adam came into the bedroom.

'George is here. He'd like to meet you.'

George McCoy! Her spirits lifted. From Adam's descriptions of the old man, he was her kind of person—zany, adventurous. She'd hoped he'd make it back before they'd have to leave so she could meet him in person. She rushed out to greet him.

George McCoy stood up when Kate came through the doors, still amazingly erect for a man his age. Piercing blue eyes under a thick thatch of silver-white hair looked into hers as he shook her hand. He was short and stocky, wearing a white sport-shirt and a loose fitting pair of shorts made of a red and white checked fabric. They looked like he'd picked them up at a small-town rummage sale twenty years ago. Eccentric, Adam had called him. Well, he certainly looked it, for being a millionaire and owning this luxurious villa.

She gave him a wide smile. 'I'm so glad to meet you!'

'It's usually only the unattached ones that say that to me with so much enthusiasm,' he said, breaking into a smile.

Kate laughed. 'I'm just dying to hear about your canoe trip. You're not looking for a job, by any chance, are you?'

He gave her a startled look, then burst out laughing. Adam rolled his eyes and grinned. 'She'll have to explain that one to you,' he said to McCoy.

'Okay, over a glass of wine.' He took Kate's elbow. 'Come with me and let's find something special.' He winked at Adam. 'I'm taking her to the dungeons. Don't come looking for us.'

The wine cellar was cool and dark, but for the rest had nothing in common with a dungeon. Bottles of wine lay on racks built along the wall and George McCoy quickly scanned the collection and selected one of the bottles.

'How's this?' He showed her the label. 'Nice little wine, good year.'

'I'm sure it is. I'm no connoisseur.'

He grinned. 'Neither am I. I just play at it for the fun of it.'

Kate followed him out, closing the door behind her.

'So,' he said, 'you have a job for me?'

'I was only joking.'

'You'd better tell me about it. If I get bored, I might just take it.'

Over a glass of wine on the terrace, she told him of her agency and the adventurous trips she took each year. He listened intently, asking questions.

'So, if you ever get bored and want to join us,' Kate said half-seriously, 'give us a call.'

'Beware,' Adam interjected. 'It's an outfit run almost exclusively by single women.'

Kate glared at him and McCoy laughed.

The old man saved the evening for her. It was hard to be depressed in his company. His energy and vitality were impressive and keen intelligence shone in the blue eyes. He came into the kitchen with them to help them cook the evening meal, teaching Kate his own special recipe for preparing the local fish she'd bought that morning. He made them laugh with his outrageous stories and she wondered secretly how much of what he told them was actually true.

He took them to the airport early the next morning and said goodbye with the invitation to come back to the villa any time they pleased.

They flew to Paris, from where Kate had booked a flight to New York and Adam one to London.

'I'll call you,' he said, kissing her head. She clung to him, forcing tears back. She watched him stride purposefully down the airport lounge until he disappeared among the other travellers.

How long this time? she wondered.

She'd never before felt so empty and alone.

Roxanne was standing on her head, feet braced against the wall, when Kate came home from a trip to Micronesia.

'Hi,' Kate said, dumping her suitcase on the floor. 'God, what a flight. There was a bomb threat in Honolulu before we even got off the ground and they unloaded us and all the luggage. It took hours.'

'All in a day's work,' Roxanne grunted. Her face was bright red. 'Adam called. He left a message on the machine.'

'Adam?' Kate felt a rush of joy and all tiredness suddenly evaporated. Hastily she shrugged out of her jacket, dropped it on a chair and rushed over to the answering machine.

There were other messages on the machine and she fast-forwarded through them impatiently until she finally heard Adam's familiar deep voice.

'Kate, this is Adam. I'm sorry, but I can't meet you in Rome on Friday. I'm in Nairobi on my way to Malindi to take over a job for one of my colleagues. He had to go home for a family emergency. One of his

kids was in a bad accident. I'll be staying at the Palm
Beach Hotel in case you want to contact me. I'm sorry
I didn't catch you home. Hope we can figure
something out later.'

'Damn, damn,' Kate muttered as she switched off
the machine. If she hadn't been delayed in Honolulu,
at least she would have been here to take the phone
call and speak to him in person. She hated this
impersonal message on a tape, his businesslike voice.
Well, that was Adam—businesslike, efficient. On the
outside, anyway. She closed her eyes, feeling a rush of
longing for him—for the touch of his fingers, the smile
in his eyes.

Roxanne lowered her feet to the floor and assumed a
more natural sitting position. She was dressed in black
tights and black and white striped leotard. Her dark
eyes looked large in the small face with its short black
hair. 'Sorry about that,' she said matter-of-factly.
'You're not having much luck.'

'I haven't seen him in over two months,' Kate
moaned, feeling deflated like a collapsed balloon. She
sagged inelegantly into a big chair.

'Two months and you still remember him?'

'Oh, shut up, Roxanne!' Wearily Kate raked her
hand through the heavy fall of her hair.

Roxanne frowned. 'You've got to understand, Kate,
that it's not going to get any better. You need
somebody stationary to come home to, not somebody
who races around the world like you do. What was
wrong with that architect or that computer scientist?'

'They were boring.'

'Well, that's a point. But so is Adam.'

'That shows how well you know him.'

'How well do *you* know him? How often have you
seen him in the last eight months? Four times? Five?

'Five.' A glorious week in the South of France, ten

days in New York, a long weekend in San Francisco, two days in Manila, passing through, another three days in New York. Twenty-five days altogether. Long enough to discover that Adam was more than just a conservative business executive in a traditional suit and tie. Long enough to find out that he was a man of substance and integrity. A man whose eyes made her heart melt and whose touch sent her quivering into heaven. Long enough to know that she loved him. Kate leaned her head back and sighed. It was an impossible situation—they were never in the same place at the same time. A relationship did not flourish well under such circumstances.

The problem was that it didn't want to die either. Like some scrawny plant that wouldn't quite give up, it kept hanging on for dear life, nourished only by occasional meetings in odd places around the world. Maybe I should be merciful and kill it off, she thought. Stop the suffering. It was a rather melodramatic thought, and she played with it for a moment.

Not see Adam any more. Forget him. There were other men in the world—doctors, lawyers, teachers, conveniently chained to one location by the nature of their professions.

But no one like Adam. Seeing him a few times a year was better than nothing. Oh, God, she groaned inwardly, I've got to be crazy.

She looked at her watch and frowned. 'What time is it in Kenya?' she asked Roxanne. 'What time is it here, for that matter? It can't be two at night with the sun shining.'

'Not unless you're in Lapland. Unfortunately this is New York. It's nine after four p.m. It's nine after twelve midnight in Kenya.' Roxanne's brain functioned like a computer. Once she'd plugged in any information it was there for immediate recall for ever after.

Kate sighed wearily. 'Too late to call. He'll be in bed.'

'Maybe not alone. Better not risk it.'

'Thanks, I needed that. You're in great form, Roxy. What are you doing here, anyway?'

'I moved back into my old room. Hope you don't mind.'

'What about Khalim?'

'*Finito*,' Roxanne said impassively. 'He didn't like my long absences. Got a bit possessive. Fooled around when I wasn't there.'

'We can't have that,' Kate said sarcastically. Roxanne treated men like disposable plates and her lack of emotional involvement always amazed Kate.

She watched Roxanne doing some contortionist exercise on the floor, her arms and legs twisted in improbable angles and curves. There was a silence for a while. Roxanne concentrated on her body. Kate watched without much interest, too tired to move and get out of the chair and take a shower. She thought of Adam, disappointment heavy in her chest. A weekend in Rome with Adam. She'd so looked forward to it. It had all worked out so well. She was due in Thailand on Tuesday next week. She'd start out early and spend the weekend with Adam in Rome, who would be on his way back from Africa. It might be weeks before they could arrange something again that was compatible with both their schedules.

Roxanne had unwound her various limbs and stood erect now, stretching. 'You look bushed, kid. Can I get you something? A cup of tea? I have something new, a special blend masterminded by Johnnie. You'll like it.'

Herbal tea. Johnnie owned a herb and spice shop

and custom-blended tea and other herbal concoctions for his customers. Kate shook her head. 'I'd rather have some regular tea, if you don't mind.' She wasn't in the mood for Roxanne's experimentations at the moment.

'Sure, no problem.'

Kate pushed herself to her feet. 'I think I'll have a quick shower first though. I'll try and stay up until eight or so before I collapse.' If she went to bed any earlier she'd be up in the middle of the night. Tomorrow there were meetings at the office all day long. She wanted to be fresh.

The hot water streaming over her face and body relaxed her, but her legs felt heavy and her body seemed made of rubber. She thought of Adam, sleeping peacefully in a hotel in Malindi on the Kenya coast. There was a stab of longing, a sudden fierce need. She wanted to be with him, to feel his arms around her, to hear his voice whispering love words in her ear. She wanted to see his face, the mouth with its corner turned up, that special gleam in his eyes when he looked at her. She wanted to run her hands over the short curly hair, to kiss him and hold him and make love. There was an ache of regret and fear.

Would it ever work?

'*You've got to understand it's not going to get any better.*'

Kate realised she was crying, the tears mingling with the water streaming down her face.

Samantha came breezing in an hour later, clutching a number of bags and packages, which she dropped on the floor. She hugged Kate.

'Nice to see you. How was your trip? Wait till you hear what happened to me in Brazil! But first let me show you what I bought. I'll put it on right now.'

She came back moments later, dressed in a flimsy white summer dress with ruffles and lace.

'Isn't it the most romantic thing you've ever seen?' she asked eagerly, swirling around on her toes, her blonde hair swinging loose around her shoulders.

Roxanne looked at Kate and rolled her eyes. Roxanne went for black and slinky. Kate grinned. 'Looks like you, Sam. Nice with that tan.' Kate didn't care for the dress, either—it wasn't her style, but it was right for Samantha with her super romantic nature. She liked ruffled curtains, embroidered sheets, sentimental poetry and elevator music, which was supposed to be soothing and relaxing. It had the opposite effect on Kate. After ten minutes of listening to the schmaltzy drivel she felt like tearing out her hair and running screaming from the room.

We're all so different, all four of us, Kate thought as she watched Roxanne and Samantha. The last member of their foursome, Becky, was married and lived in an apartment not far away. Becky was the quiet, introspective one, Samantha the romantic, Roxanne the cynic, and Kate . . . well, Kate wasn't sure how to characterise herself. Extrovert, happy-go-lucky maybe? She enjoyed life. She enjoyed her work, travelling, meeting people. She liked being independent and free. Free of the nine-to-five routine of an office. It was what the four of them had in common— the desire to do something different, to use their knowledge of far-away places, their experience with things foreign. Their fathers had been, and still were, employed by the State Department. They'd all grown up in various foreign locations. The four of them had met in college, gravitating towards each other because of their common backgrounds.

Now, five years after graduation, they were still together, running a speciality travel service, 'catering to the adventurous and discriminating traveller', the brochures read. They did not deal in the routine organised tours to familiar places. They sought out the unusual, the adventurous, tailoring vacations and tours to the individual needs of their clients. They'd found it a lucrative business and they'd done more than well.

Dinner was a vegetarian dish concocted by Roxanne, who was into health food and exercise. They talked about work, but Kate could not keep her eyes open and sat practically sleeping upright in her chair. By seven-thirty she gave up the struggle and went to bed. Someone, probably Samantha, had made up the bed with fresh sheets.

Her sleep was deep and exhausted without dreams, but didn't last through the night. She surfaced from sleep a little after two. She gazed around in the dark, wide awake. Her own room, familiar and recognisable, even in the dark. The apartment was silent. She lay still in the bed, moving only to wipe the hair out of her face. What day was it? Tuesday. Don't think, she said to herself. Go back to sleep.

Adam. Rome. She tossed and turned, thinking of Adam. Three o'clock. It was eleven in the morning in Kenya. He would probably not be in his hotel room. Well, maybe he was. He could be working, writing his report.

She raised herself up on an elbow and switched on the bedside lamp. Then she picked up the phone and dialled the operator. She didn't have the number for the Palm Beach Hotel in Malindi, but they found it for her. Palm Beach Hotel—the name alone was so devoid of originality. Every tropical or semi-tropical coast in the world sported a Palm Beach Hotel.

Some time later she had the hotel reception on the line.

'I'm calling from New York. I'd like to speak to Mr Adam Cooper, please. I don't know his room number.'

'Room three-oh-two. One moment, please.'

The phone rang. She closed her eyes and held her breath. It was silly to hope he'd be there. He'd he out talking to the city council or a bank or some local businessmen. The phone was answered almost immediately and her heart gave a giant leap.

'Hello. Cooper here.' Short, businesslike.

'Adam? It's Kate.'

'Kate!' The tone of his voice warmed. 'Did you get my message?'

'Yes.'

Static crackled over the line and she missed his next words. 'What did you say?'

'I said, I'm sorry. There was nothing I could do.'

'I know, I understand. Can you hear me all right?'

'Yes.' His tone was impatient.

'I've been trying to think of what to do. I'll be gone when you get back. I'll be in Thailand for a month. I may be able to get an extra week . . .' A burst of static interrupted her again. 'This is a lousy line!' she shouted. 'Adam, what's your schedule?'

'Kate, I don't know now! It's all being rearranged because of this. Listen, Kate, I can't talk now. I'm in the middle of a meeting.'

'In your room?'

'Yes.'

'I'm sorry I disturbed you,' she said coolly, feeling an unreasonable anger wash over her. 'There's never any time for us, is there? Not to see each other, not even to talk on the telephone.'

'Kate . . .'

'Oh, it's all right, Adam. See you around some time.' She slammed down the phone, her disillusionment so acute, she was shaking with it.

I should have known, she thought. *We're not good for each other. There's no way this is ever going to work unless I give up everything.* The thought made her crawl with anxiety. How could she give up everything she had worked so hard for these last years? How could she give up the work she loved? But in her life now there was only marginal time for love. All she and Adam had was a long-distance love affair—magic times of exquisite delight punctuated by long stretches of emptiness and painful yearning.

What they had was more than just the pleasures of their bodies. More than anything she savoured the moments after—the sweetness and the tenderness that followed the session. It was the laughter they shared, the hours of just being together, of talking and discovering the hidden treasures in the mind and heart of each other. He knew more about her than anyone had ever known.

She pressed the palms of her hand against her eyes. 'I can't bear it,' she moaned. '*I can't bear it!*'

'Kate?'

She looked up. Roxanne was standing in the doorway, wearing a black sleep shirt. She carried her obsession for black straight into the bedroom with her. Kate stared at her. 'Why are you not asleep?'

'Because you woke me up with your shouting.'

'I'm sorry. I was talking to Adam and the line was bad.' She grabbed the pillow from behind her and squeezed it hard against her.

'What's the matter, Kate?'

'He didn't have time to talk to me! He was having a goddamned *meeting* in his room! Planning another one of his assembly-line hotels, no doubt. He was all businesslike efficiency and I hate it! I hate it!' She ranted on for a few more minutes, spewing her anger, her disappointment.

'Don't yell at me,' Roxanne said mildly.

'Who else am I going to yell at? You can take it. You swallow a handful of Stresstabs every morning.'

Roxanne laughed. 'Maybe you could use some right now. Come on, I'll make us some tea.'

There was nothing to do but scratch Rome. Instead, she flew to Tunis to visit her parents for the weekend before going on to Bangkok to meet up with her tour group.

The three weeks they spent in the rural north of the country passed uneventfully, at least from Kate's point of view. During the days she thought of Adam, at night she dreamed of him. A mixture of resentment and fear began to take up permanent residence in her mind.

Thailand was one of Kate's favourite places. Possibly because she'd lived there as a teenager for some time and had happy memories of the place. She didn't feel happy now. She lay on her hotel bed in Bangkok, having handed over her group to a local guide who would show them all the glittery golden temples and Buddhas—the Golden Buddha, the Reclining Buddha, the Emerald Buddha, which wasn't made of emerald at all, but jasper. Tomorrow a junior employee of the agency would escort the group back to the States. Kate would travel back on her own.

She closed her eyes, opening them again with a start when the telephone rang. She picked up the receiver.

'Hello?'

'Miss Flannigan? Reception here. There's someone here to see you. Mr Cooper.'

For a moment the breath stuck in her throat. She closed her eyes. 'I ... er ... tell him I'll be right down.'

CHAPTER SIX

SHE rushed into the bathroom, looked at herself in the mirror and groaned. She'd just had a shower and washed her hair. She had nothing on but a short, cotton bathrobe and a towel around her head and her face was scrubbed clean of make-up. Ripping off the towel, she picked up the hair dryer and turned it on full blast. Giving up when her hair was only half dry, she began to apply eyeshadow, mascara, blusher, to be stopped in the middle of her efforts by a knock on the door.

'Who is it?' she called, walking into the narrow passage outside the bathroom.

'Adam.'

Her heart began to thud wildly. She opened the door. It had been nearly three months since she'd last seen him, one since her phone call to Kenya. The sight of him turned her knees to water. He looked so good, so big and solid and strong. The brown eyes looked at her with warm intensity, the mouth curled in a faint smile. Her eyes raced over him, taking in everything—the broad shoulders under the green sportshirt, the long legs outlined in the lightweight slacks. Her mouth went dry and she swallowed, bracing herself mentally.

'Come in,' she said huskily. 'I'm sorry I'm not ready, but I wasn't expecting you and when they called me from downstairs I . . .'

'It's all right, Kate. How are you?' He advanced into the room, scrutinising her face.

'Oh, I'm fine. Look around. Fancy hotel. Great bed, good food, swimming pool, the works.'

'I thought you didn't like to stay in places like this.'

'When did I say that?'

'On a number of occasions.'

'Oh, well, now and then I have no choice.'

He gave a crooked smile. 'Suffering through it, are we?'

Her stomach felt hollow with longing, yet she suppressed the urge to come close, touch him, throw herself into his arms, smell the warm, familiar scent of him.

'Why are you here?'

'To see you, of course.'

The bitterness and anger she had nursed over the last month came bubbling to the surface. 'I didn't think you cared to see me any more.'

'Don't, Kate,' he said softly.

'Don't what? You didn't even want to *talk* to me when I called you in Malindi!'

'Kate, I was in the middle of a meeting with some guys I'd had a lot of trouble trying to see. You've got to understand that.'

'I don't understand anything! Oh, why did I have to get started with this whole sorry affair! Why did I go out with you? I knew from the beginning it wasn't going to work out! Why did you have to sit next to me on that plane?'

'Because the agent assigned me the seat,' he said levelly.

'Hah! I bet you slipped her something to get it!'

'As a matter of fact, I didn't.'

'You want me to believe that? You want me to believe it was a *coincidence* you had the seat next to mine?'

'I only said I didn't bribe the agent. I didn't have to. All I did was use a little charm. And please, Kate, let's not get all melodramatic about this. I didn't go through all the trouble to get here just to argue with you about what seat I sat in nine or ten months ago.'

'Well, you wasted your time! I'm leaving tomorrow morning.'

'No, you're not.' He pushed his hands in his pockets and surveyed her with a small smile.

'You want to see my tickets?'

'You don't have to be back in New York until next week, Thursday, for the annual meeting. All the other appointments on your schedule have been cancelled or postponed.'

She arched her brows. 'Is that so? And how did that happen?'

'I called your office and arranged it. Becky was very understanding.'

She was bereft of speech. She stared at him as anger raced through her. 'You what?' she asked at last, nearly choking on the words.

'I called Becky and told her our predicament.'

'How *dare* you interfere in my life like that! Whoever gave you the permission to arrange my life for me?' She was shaking with rage, the heat of it flushing her face. He had called her office, talked to Becky and rearranged her schedule all without her knowledge. It was unthinkable, unheard of!

'Kate, I wanted to see you. I had to do *something*. There was no way for me to contact you. You were incommunicado and you know it.'

'That still doesn't give you the right to do what you did! Why didn't you rearrange your own damn schedule? Or is that one too sacrosanct to fiddle with?'

'I did change it. I took a week off.'

'I'm touched! And you can spend it with the Buddhas, for all I care! I'm leaving tomorrow morning, as planned!' She whirled around, clutching the robe to her chest with trembling hands. 'Now get out of here!'

She should have known better than to say that. His grip on her upper arms was like steel and anger blazed in his eyes.

'Kate,' he said in a dangerously soft tone, 'don't you talk to me that way. I'm not leaving until I'm ready to go.'

She glared at him. 'Suit yourself. Now let go of me!'

His mouth twisted bitterly. 'I came here to hold you,' he said quietly, dropping his hands from her arms. The anger was gone from his eyes, and she stared at him for a moment before turning her back on him. All the anger flowed out of her and an overwhelming sorrow took over. Tears flooded her eyes and she stood in front of the wardrobe, groping blindly for something to wear. It was an agonising effort not to make a sound and give away her tears. I can't stand it any more, she thought. I can't stand not seeing him. It's not his fault. Why do I blame him for it? Why am I so angry with him? Why do I feel so damned helpless?

She grabbed a dress at random and on the way to the bathroom she passed the long mirror attached to the wall. His reflection was a blurry shape and she realised he could see her, too.

'Kate . . .?'

She felt his arms around her and the comfort of his touch broke her restraint and a sob broke loose, and then another.

'What's the matter, Kate?'

She shook her head. 'I don't know,' she muttered thickly, resting her face against the broad shoulder, feeling the familiar, hard length of him close to her. 'I wanted to see you. I was so disappointed when you cancelled our weekend in Rome. And then that awful phone call. I thought everything was falling apart.'

'I called back the next day. Cost me half a night's

sleep. They said at your office you'd left for Tunis.
Was that true? Or was it another story by that sweet
little secretary who doesn't know how to lie?'

'It was true. I went to see my parents.' She'd moped
around the white villa the entire weekend until her
mother had finally got out of her what the trouble was.

'It sounds like you love him,' she'd said calmly.
'I've never seen you so worked up over a man before.'

'I don't want to love him!'

Her mother laughed. 'Unfortunately, that's not a
decision you make intellectually.'

'Well, what can I do? Go on as we are and see each
other once every other month?'

'Obviously that isn't working out very well.'

'I'm not going to give up my career and live in a New
York apartment waiting for him to come home to me!'

'There must be other solutions, Kate. Why do you
always see everything in extremes?'

Other solutions. Like what? If only she could see
some. Here she was in Adam's arms and all she could
do was fight with him and cry. She'd never felt so
helpless before. She'd never been so weepy in her life.
She drew in a shaky breath. 'I'm sorry. I didn't mean
to crack up like that. I haven't been my old cheerful
self lately.'

His lips were trailing a path from her neck to her
mouth. She clung to him, feeling sweet desire drown
out her fear and anger. He pressed her close against
him, kissing her with unrestrained passion and she felt
a quiver run down her back. His kisses were magic—
they had been from the very beginning. It was always
like this—this helpless frenzy fired by the long
absences. It was like a spell, a trance, a loss of sanity.
Nothing mattered when she was in his arms.
Nothing . . .

*   *   *

She couldn't believe it was always that easy. She lay in his arms after they'd made love with hungry abandon, wondering what it was that made her lose all her self-control when she was in his arms. After all those weeks, all that pent-up yearning for him was finally released. She'd once thought that when they weren't together she could just turn some mental switch in her mind and go into hibernation. No Adam—no loving, no tender touches, no passionate nights. Well, she hadn't switched herself off—merely blocked a running tap. It was wonderful and it frightened her senseless. I'm addicted to him, she thought, examining the face close to her. His eyes were closed. Thick lashes, dark eyebrows. He looked very relaxed, very peaceful, no sharp angles or lines. Was he asleep? She longed to kiss the closed eyes, but didn't want to disturb him. Addicted. It was a strange thought, yet it described her feelings for him very well. I'm obsessed and I can't help myself, she thought. I love him to distraction. I'm in trouble.

Deep trouble. She'd said goodbye to other men, but how could she ever let Adam go? He was in her blood. It was so good to be with him. With him she didn't feel restrained or restricted, didn't have to play some role and pretend to be something she wasn't. She'd never felt so close to another man.

You don't have to let him go, her inner voice said.

Then what? Live like this? This is no way. It'll kill me. Seeing him only once or twice every few months is not enough. She put her mouth against the smooth skin of his shoulder. He didn't move. She could feel the slow, steady thudding of his heart.

So, give up your job. Do something else. Stay put in New York, like Becky.

But she wasn't Becky. After her marriage, Becky

had taken over running the business in New York. The agency didn't need two managers, although expanding the business was something they had discussed and a new office position would probably be needed and developed.

I don't want to be in the office all the time, she thought angrily. I want to be where the people are. I want to go places. I can't sit in New York all year round! She wanted adventure and excitement, tropical beaches and primitive villages and exotic food. Another obsession, she thought wryly. Oh, damn! Why did life have to be so complicated?

Adam stirred. The eyelashes fluttered and opened. 'What's wrong?' he asked. 'You're all tense.'

She sighed. 'Nothing.'

He propped himself up on one elbow and scrutinised her face with half-closed eyes. 'Don't lie to me, little girl. I can feel it in your luscious limbs.' He slowly stroked her thigh. 'And you were perfectly relaxed not so many minutes ago.'

She forced a sunny smile. 'Your magic touch.'

'Mmm . . . Maybe I'd better try it again.' With one finger he drew lazy circles around her breast. 'You're not mad at me any more?'

She shook her head, feeling her nipple tingle into life. His eyes were laughing into hers, then slowly, deliberately he lowered his gaze.

'Look at that,' he said, 'magic.' He bent down his head and his warm, moist mouth captured the nipple and tickled it with his tongue.

She gave an exaggerated moan and let out a lazy sigh. 'I'm relaxed now.'

'Looks more like excited to me.'

She laughed. 'You're awful.'

'I'm *wonderful*.'

'That, too.'

He brushed her mouth with his lips. 'Let's get energised and we'll make magic for the rest of the night.'

'Energised?'

'Food. F-o-o-d.'

'Okay, that's good. Food is good.'

'Room service?'

She made a face. 'Yuk. I want real food.'

He laughed softly, shaking his head. 'You're a twenty-four-carat snob. Have I ever told you?'

She grinned. 'Yep. Many times. Any other complaints?'

'You're also a twenty-four-carat lover. Where did you learn that?'

'I took a correspondence course.'

He laughed out loud, a warm, delighted sound coming from deep in his chest. 'That explains it. And to think I've been wondering about all those lovers you must have had.'

She played with the curls on his chest. 'And what about you? Where did you learn to do your magic?'

'I've just a natural talent.'

She nodded solemnly. 'Of course, I should have known. And now, can I get up and dress?'

He lay back, hands behind his head, and watched her as she slipped on champagne-coloured panties and bra, satiny things with lace around the edges. She stepped into high-heeled sandals and struck a seductive pose. 'The Maidenform woman,' she whispered. 'You never know where she'll show up.'

He leaped off the bed with the sleek agility of a tiger going for his prey, grabbed her around the waist and tossed her on the bed. He lay down on top of her, holding her down, and ravaged her with kisses, leaving her gasping for air when he finally raised his head.

'Please don't!' she whimpered, feigning panic. 'Please, not like this!'

His eyes glittered. 'You asked for it!'

'Oh, but I didn't mean it!'

He tugged at her panties, grinning devilishly. 'Oh, yes you did. And you're going to get it!'

She squirmed. 'Please, no! Please, please!'

'Please, please, yes!'

She struggled some more, which didn't do anything to cool either of them down, until she dissolved into laughter and grew limp. He slid off the flimsy scrap of fabric and flung it across the room. She didn't move, just looked at the bronzed face hovering above her, feeling desire rush madly through her veins.

The eyes narrowed slightly. 'Give up?'

'They say the best thing to do is not to fight it.' She closed her eyes and sighed wearily. 'Go ahead, do your thing. I'll lie back and think of New York.'

That got to him. 'You *what*?'

She shook with laughter. 'I was taking liberties with the quote "lie back and think of England."'

'Never heard of it.' His mouth moved down, dotting her stomach with warm, moist kisses, while his hands held her hips so she couldn't move.

'You haven't? Where have you been?' It took an effort to speak, to think, to breathe.

He lifted his face and white teeth gleamed as he grinned at her. 'Not with anybody who lay back and thought of England.'

She didn't doubt it for a moment. It was impossible to remain untouched by him. Her blood sang, her body was on fire. It was impossible to lie still. 'Presumably, it's the advice Englishwomen living in the colonies gave their daughters on their wedding nights.'

He groaned, rolling his eyes. 'And that's what you're going to do? Forget it, baby, you haven't got it in you.' He slid his body up over hers. He ran his tongue around the edge of her mouth and her lips parted, inviting him in. Her arms slid around his back and she made little noises of delight.

They came together in a frenzy of passion. No finesse, no long, lingering caresses, nothing but wild fever.

He rolled back, collapsing with a groan. 'My God,' he gasped, 'this can't be healthy. No wonder fate keeps us apart.'

Kate laughed breathlessly. 'You've got incredible powers of recuperation, I must say.'

'It's all part of the magic.' He took a ragged breath. 'You want to try again?'

Kate groaned. 'Oh, please have mercy on me! Let's get out of here before I starve to death.'

'It's only six o'clock.'

'I didn't eat lunch.' She got off the bed and he followed her into the bathroom.

She turned and faced him, eyebrows arched. 'I beg your pardon?'

'I like communal showers.' He leaned over and turned on the taps. 'Get in.'

'Oh, well, if you insist.' Gingerly she stepped into the shiny bath. 'Ouch! It's too hot!'

He adjusted the taps. 'I thought you liked it hot.'

'Oh, Adam, how vulgar! I didn't think you had in it you!'

'There's a lot you don't know about me,' he commented with a leer. He climbed into the bath with her, closing his eyes as he stood with his head in the streaming water. 'What kind of food do you want to eat? French, Bulgarian, Korean, Japanese, Thai?'

'When in Thailand, eat as the Thai do.'

'Good idea. So where do we go? Kreur Taow? Thon Tum Rub? Sala Thai?' He began to soap her breasts with slow, sensuous movements.

'You must have been to Bangkok before.'

'Often enough.'

She took a deep breath, looking down at his hands on her breasts. 'I think they're clean now.'

'I didn't get the rest of you.' He slid his hand down her front and massaged her stomach. 'So where do you want to go?'

'Not Sala Thai. They have classical dancing. They used to have, anyway.'

'Don't you like Thai dancing?' His fingers were wandering lower and she slapped his hand away. 'Gee, you're a lech! Don't you ever have enough? And no, I don't like classical dancing. It's so damned slow, it makes me itch all over. And those women dressed up to look like dolls in all their finery. Ever noticed those nails they put on? Five inches long, I swear.'

'I like the way they move,' he said, sliding his hands over to her hips and making her sway. 'Very sensual, very sexy. And those costumes are quite spectacular.'

'Go see them without me.' She wiped the mass of wet hair out of her face.

'I'd rather be with you.'

'Well, in that case, I know a very nice little place. You have to sit on cushions though, Thai style.'

'I think I can manage.' He put his wet face against her. 'Kiss me?'

They stood together in the streaming water, slippery bodies sliding against each other. Out of necessity it was a brief kiss and she drew away, gasping. 'I'll drown. I'll promise you a better one, later.' She stepped out of the bath tub carefully, and with one of the smaller towels, squeezed the water out of her hair before wrapping a big one around her body.

'Where are you staying?' she asked. 'At the Crown Hotel on Rama Road?'

'Yes.' He was drying himself vigorously with another one of the thick, white towels. For a moment she relished the enjoyment of watching him. Muscles rippled in the brown arms as he rubbed his chest, drying the wet hair into fuzzy curls. An impressive physique, with the wide-set shoulders, the flat stomach, the long, muscular legs. And intelligence and charm and a sense of humour finishing it all off nicely. So, she said to herself, what else do you want?

His eyes met hers and she batted her lashes at him, turned and swung out of the bathroom to get dressed.

The restaurant was hidden at the back of an unalluring *soy*, a dark little alley, that suddenly led into a beautiful Oriental garden complete with an illuminated pond full of lotus flowers. The restaurant was small and dimly lit, decorated in exotic Oriental style and perfumed with the spicy fragrances of Thai cooking. They took off their shoes as they entered, leaving them in the entry way with those of the other customers. They were studied with brief, polite curiosity as they were escorted to their table. Obviously, *farang* customers were not a daily occurrence.

'Very nice,' said Adam as they lowered themselves on the cushions at the low table. 'What would you like to drink? Rice wine?'

Kate grimaced. 'No thanks. Tastes like alcoholic corn syrup. Too sweet for me. I'll just have water.'

The food, when it came, was a feast. They'd ordered rice and a number of smaller dishes— vegetables, chicken, beef curry, egg and meat fritters, fish—the bowls grouped in a semi-circle around their plates. Kate eyed the food feverishly and Adam laughed.

'You look ready for attack.'

'I am.' She spooned a heap of rice on her plate, then added some food from each of the various bowls.

'Don't eat yourself sick,' Adam warned, watching her dig in.

She swallowed delicately, feigning an expression of distaste. 'Heavens no, that's so low class.' She pushed more food on to her spoon with her fork, Thai style, and brought it to her mouth.

'Phew,' she said, after she'd chewed and swallowed. 'This is the real stuff. Is my hair on fire?' She drank some water to cool down her burning throat.

'As a matter of fact it is, but I don't think it's the hot pepper. Tell me, what have you been doing up north with your group? What kind of group was it this time?'

'Theology students.'

'And what did you do with theology students in the north of Thailand?'

'We went to elephant school,' she said, smiling sedately, her spoon hovering close to her mouth.

Incredulity flickered briefly in the brown eyes. 'Right. The place where they train elephants to work,' he stated. 'What did you do? Take on an apprentice-ship for three weeks? Maybe I'm dense, but I don't quite see the connection.'

She chewed her food and swallowed. 'There isn't any.' She grinned. 'I was only saying it for effect. The elephant school was a side trip. The main purpose of the tour was to visit the hill tribes and observe and study animism. Fascinating you know, all that stuff about spirits and how to ward off the evil ones with spirit houses and altars and totems and fertility symbols, and all kinds of other magic things.'

Between bites, she told him more about the trip. The food was disappearing quickly and so was her hunger. She sighed when she finally put down her

poon and fork. 'That was good. Tell me, how is
Nicky these days? How is he doing in school?'
Adam's interest in the boy had not waned over the
months, Kate knew. His affections had only grown.
No matter how busy Adam was when he was back in
New York, there was always time for Nicky.

He smiled a crooked smile. 'He's doing very well.
Can't wait till he can read real books. He wants to get
his own library card.'

'Pretty smart kid, right?'

'Yes, I think so.' The smile faded and he frowned.
I just wish I could do more for him. That school he
goes to isn't very good.'

'If he's bright, he'll make it,' she said lightly.

'I'm not sure that's necessarily true. I want him to
have the stimulation he needs.' He toyed with his fork,
pushing a grain of rice around on his plate.

'You'll make a good father one day,' she said.

He looked up, smiling faintly. 'I'd like to think so.'
His eyes held hers and she knew she'd made a mistake.

He reached across the table and took her hand.
'What about us, Kate?'

She averted her eyes and gazed down on the big
hand covering hers on the table. 'I don't know,' she
said huskily.

'I don't see enough of you,' he said. 'You're in my
mind all the time. I want you all the time and you're
not there. I sleep in all these empty beds, and it
doesn't feel right.'

Her heart beat a nervous rhythm. 'I know.'

'We'll have to make some choices and decisions.'

The silence screamed in her ears.

'Kate?'

'Yes. I . . . I suppose so.'

There was a silence and she could feel his eyes on
her, looking into her, probing.

'Kate,' he said at last, 'I want a wife. I wan
children.'

Her heart felt like a rock suspended in her ches
Breathing was difficult—it seemed impossible to forc
the air out. She slipped her hand away from under hi
and clasped it around the other in her lap.

'I don't know what I want.'

'What are you afraid of, Kate?'

A hundred things. Afraid of losing her freedom. O
making a commitment to another person. Of adjustin,
to another life. Of making the wrong choices. Ever
fibre in her body grew rigid just at the thought of it
No matter how she hated the long separations, n
matter how she longed for him when they were apart
she wasn't ready for this discussion.

She gave him a pleading look. 'Let's not talk abou
it now, Adam, please.'

His eyes looked directly into hers, holding her gaze
'We'll have to talk about it sometime, Kate. We can'
keep ignoring the situation. We can't go on the way w
have. We have the problem of conflicting careers. W
have to face it.'

Conflicting careers. There was no mystery i
solving that problem, was there? A number of othe
men had pointed out the solution to her. Give up hers
find something else. There were still a lot of mal
chauvinists around. After all, she was a woman, and i
wasn't as if she was doing anything particularl
important, such as being a lawyer or a doctor savin,
people from either social or physical evils. Her wor
was rather frivolous and she'd have to give it u
sooner or later anyway, if she wanted to raise
family . . .

She was suddenly uncomfortably hot. She put he
napkin down on the table. 'Let's just get out of here
Adam.'

'Let me get the bill.'

He was not happy, she could tell. The light had gone out of his eyes. His mouth looked strained, with grooves running down from the corners.

Oh, damn, she thought miserably. Damn! Damn!

In the taxi back to her hotel, she tried to lighten the mood, chatting about her next tour in Sierra Leone in West Africa, and about the village the agency had bought in the Dordogne in France.

'You bought an entire village?'

'The whole entire thing.' She grinned. 'Eight houses, and not a soul living in them. A hamlet, really, a ghost hamlet. Roxanne discovered it, literally. On a biking tour. Leave it to her to come up with something like that. It was all overgrown with brambles and the grass was ten feet high . . .' She stopped as she saw Adam's eyebrows shoot up in sceptical disbelief. 'Well,' she amended, 'maybe it was eight feet. Five? Three?'

He nodded. 'That's probably more like it.'

'Anyway, we're going to fix up the cottages and rent them out. The Dordogne is a gorgeous area of France, very picturesque with lots of quaint villages and churches and castles. Ever been there?'

'No.'

'Well, how do you know how high the grass grows if you've never been there!'

'An educated guess, taking into consideration the location and the climate of the country.'

'Yes, sir, professor, of course.'

She searched for his hand, feeling a certain reticence in him, a distance. He was perturbed because she'd refused to talk. She was too afraid to talk, to hear the words she didn't want to hear, to make decisions she didn't want to make.

'Adam?' she said, after a silence. 'I'd like to get out of town. I know an island off the East coast, in the China sea. A friend of mine has a cottage there. It's beautiful and very quiet and not many foreigners know about it. Would you like to go there for a few days? It's called Koh Santisuk—Peace Island.'

He squeezed her hand. 'Sounds nice. Let's do that.'

She closed her eyes briefly, feeling relief wash over her. Peace Island, here we come, she thought.

Through half-closed eyes, Kate watched Adam come towards her across the sand. She had a good view of him and she let her gaze linger unashamedly on his near-naked body, enjoying the sight of it, the lean strength of it, the pure male beauty of it. Short white swimming trunks contrasted starkly with his deeply tanned torso. Even walking in the loose sand, his movements seemed effortless. A golden demi-god—perfect, beautiful.

Yet he was different from the other handsome men she'd met. He was not preoccupied with his physical appearance, as so many of them seemed to be. He dressed conventionally rather than drawing attention to himself with flashy clothes or the latest designer fashions. He had a stark male appeal, a magnetism that was hard to ignore, yet he seemed to be unimpressed by it. His confidence seemed to come from an inner source rather than from conceit over his good looks. What was absent in Adam was the *Here-I-come-aren't-I-gorgeous* syndrome. She liked it. She liked it very much.

In one flowing movement he sat down next to her on the bamboo mat.

'*Pai-nai*,' she said.

'Hi.'

'You're supposed to say *pai dern-lenh*.'

'*Pai dern-lenh,*' he said obediently. He ruffled her hair. 'You look like a burning bush.'

They'd arrived on the island only an hour earlier, found the cottage and had decided to take a swim before going in search of lunch.

The island was small, boasted no resort hotels, no fancy restaurants, no swimming pools. A sprinkling of Thais from Bangkok came here for rest and relaxation and some had built small houses along the beach or hidden further away on the hills. *Farang* tourists did not come here. Life was too primitive and no Western food was available.

'Why aren't you in the water?' Adam asked.

'I was waiting for you.' He had insisted on unpacking first and hanging his clothes up. Kate had dug out her swimsuit and left the rest for later. She had no patience for unpacking when outside the blue-green ocean beckoned with white-crested breakers. The beach with the tall coconut palms shading the silvery sand was too much of a temptation. She couldn't get out there fast enough, smell the salty water, feel the breeze against her bare skin.

'Oh, Adam,' she'd said, 'forget the dumb suitcase! Look outside! It's paradise out there!'

'I'll only be a few minutes, Kate,' he said with maddening calm. 'Paradise can wait.' He took out some shirts and put them on a shelf.

Kate closed the suitcase and sat down on top of it, crossing her legs yoga style. Wearing nothing but a skimpy green bikini, she knew she made a rather silly picture, like some ad in a travel magazine. Adam turned and came towards her and she looked at him defiantly. 'Don't be so stuffy, Adam! Live dangerously, break your precious routine and come swimming with me now.'

He wasted no effort on words, but lifted her bodily

off the suitcase and dumped her unceremoniously on the bed. She grabbed at his shoulders and he lost his balance and half-fell on top of her.

'You're not going to win this one,' he whispered, his face almost touching hers. He disentangled himself from her grasp, his strength no match for hers, and calmly opened the suitcase again and continued unpacking.

He was not to be persuaded. She should have known. Adam *always* unpacked as soon as he arrived anywhere and Peace Island in the China Sea was no exception.

Well, it hadn't taken him very long, she had to admit. She jumped up, grabbing his left hand. 'Come on, let's go.' They raced toward the water.

'It's warm! It's wonderful!' Kate yelled, splashing through it with the eagerness of a child. 'Come on, let's catch that wave!' She jumped in right before it broke and went sailing back to the beach, Adam following.

They swam and surfed and played for an hour. 'I'm hungry,' she said at last, putting her arms around his neck and giving him a salty kiss. His short curly hair was full of silvery drops glittering in the sun. In the water his body felt cool and strong and slippery.

'Me, too,' he said, pressing her close against him. 'God, I want you!'

'I can tell.' She grinned, secretly pleased at the effect she was having on him. 'Here? Now? It'll be a challenge.'

He gently bit her lower lip. 'No, not here for the world to see, you little pervert.'

Kate glanced around. 'Not a soul in the water,' she defended.

'But half a dozen people walking along the beach. Besides, we'd probably drown.'

She grinned. 'What a way to go!'

Adam rolled his eyes and groaned. He reached for
her hand. 'Come on, let's get back.'

'The thing to do is to look past the dirt,' Kate
instructed as they sat down at the none-too-clean table
in the open roadside restaurant. 'We Americans have a
phobia about germs and bacteria. We're so squeaky
clean we've destroyed our natural immunities to plain
old dirt. No wonder everybody always gets sick when
they go abroad.'

'But not you, of course,' said Adam drily, glancing
around him with interest.

Kate gave him a smug grin. 'Not me. Dirt has no
argument with me. I never get sick. I eat everything
and my system says thank-you-very-much and
processes it without complaints.'

A pregnant dog wandered in from outside and
settled herself down next to Adam's chair, gazing up
at him with such a look of devotion that Kate had to
laugh. Adam scowled at the mongrel. 'Make yourself
at home,' he invited darkly.

'You have to admit,' said Kate, 'this is not your run-
of-the-mill fast food place. This is different. Nothing
artificial or plastic about it. It's the real thing.'

'Except for this.' Adam nodded at the empty Coca
Cola bottle with a pink plastic rose in it that graced the
table.

Kate smiled brightly. 'Well, you know what I
mean.' She picked up the menu, a typed piece of paper
in a sticky plastic cover. The dishes were listed in both
Thai and English, and it was an impressive list
considering the size of the restaurant.

Restaurant—too pretentious a name for this modest
little eating house, Kate thought, surveying the place.
It was nothing more than a roof held up by bamboo

poles. It had a view of the beach and cool sea breeze
wafted freely in from the Indian Ocean. About ten
rickety tables were spaced around at neat intervals,
each decorated with a dusty plastic rose in an attempt
at chic. The thought behind the plastic flower
intrigued her. Exotic flowers and bushes bloomed
luxuriantly everywhere on the island—hibiscus,
frangipani, orchids, and a hundred others she didn't
know by name. The place itself was surrounded by
blooming bougainvillaea, and a lush green creeper
with orange blossoms trailed along a disintegrating
bamboo fence. So why a plastic rose on the table?

A noise attracted her attention. A naked child sat in
the dirt and played with a plastic racing car, growling
in imitation of a revving engine. The dog, too, had
heard the noise and lifted up her head. With laborious
movements she came to her feet and waddled out to
investigate further. Smiling, Kate returned her
attention to the menu.

'How about some Kai Tom Kha? Thai chili
chicken?' she suggested. 'Or, let's see, grilled crab
with hot sauce. That's pretty messy though. You have
to eat it with your fingers. I don't object to that
myself—the child in me likes to get messy. Food and
sauce all over my face and hands, not to speak of my
hair . . .' She stopped, grinning at Adam, who gave her
a long-suffering look.

'Don't be so stuffy. You look just like my father.'

His face broke into a grin. 'God forbid I should ever
have a child like you.' He picked up his own menu and
studied it.

Better not marry me then, she retorted silently. *You
might just end up with one, or who knows, even two or
three.* Why was she thinking things like that? She
stared blindly at the list of dishes.

After a moment, Adam tossed the menu on the

table. 'I think I'll have the curried shrimp. Seafood seems to be the speciality here.'

'Fresh from the boats every morning.' She smiled brightly, forcing back uneasy thoughts.

A barefoot waitress in jeans and a hot-pink T-shirt came to take their orders. Her heavy black hair hung in a braid down her back and luscious dark eyes smiled at them in friendly welcome. Her fractured English was a joy to the ear.

The local beer they ordered was cold and refreshing, and Kate leaned back in her creaky rattan chair, sighing with contentment. 'This is the life, you know. Sun and sea and the best food in the world. Nirvana.'

A loud wail broke the peaceful silence. Outside a woman was whacking the naked child with a green sarong. The boy danced around, crying, trying to escape the swinging sarong.

'Nirvana?' Adam enquired.

'Oh, well, almost.' She gazed outside, squinting against the bright glare, taking in the pink and purple bougainvillaea drooping heavily to the ground, the sea glittering in the midday sun, the tall coconut palms shading the beach. It was the stuff dreams were made of. Even after all the places she had seen, a scene like this still pleased her. She thought of living in a New York apartment year-around—the winters when everything was hard and grey and frozen; the summers, when even the steel and concrete seemed to melt in the simmering heat. *Don't think,* she admonished herself. *Live for the moment.*

The exotic surroundings did not encourage worrying and she enjoyed her lunch, eating her peppery crab with relish, but managing to stay relatively clean. The meal finished, they strolled back to the cottage. The sun was hot and straight overhead and the steamy heat combined with the beer floating around in her bloodstream made her feel drowsy. An afternoon nap was definitely in order. When the worst of the heat was gone they could go for a swim in the ocean.

A small van rumbled by on the dusty road. Kate caught sight of two young Buddhist monks in orange robes, their heads shaven bald, sitting serenely on one of the benches in the open back. The vehicle was painted in bright stripes of blue and green and orange. The back contained two long benches for transporting passengers. Similar vans, all with their own bright designs, careened all over the island and were a popular form of public transport.

'If I ever buy a car,' Kate announced, 'I'll have it painted like one of those. Orange, turquoise and yellow, I think. It would brighten the City of New York, don't you think?'

He nodded solemnly, his eyes laughing. 'It would do that.'

They passed some rice paddies where a farmer was at work with a buffalo-drawn plough, and further on a fruit stand by the road displayed heaps of pineapple, papayas, durians, coconuts and other fruits. They stopped and bought some bananas to snack on later, joking with the vendor about the desirability of the durian. The ugly, spiky green fruit had the foulest imaginable smell, but the Thais loved the sweet taste.

'This might not be a bad location for a hotel,' Adam remarked casually as they walked on.

'Don't you go getting any ideas now!' Kate threatened. 'I brought you here in good faith. This place is still relatively unspoiled and I like it that way. They don't need any resort hotels. Anybody who wants to come here can come. All the fruit and fish you can eat for a pittance and perfectly adequate cottages for rent.'

'If you're willing to sleep without air-conditioning

nd do without swimming pools and tennis courts and
amburgers and . . .'

Kate stopped and glared at him, taking off her
sunglasses to give him the full benefit of the fire in her
eyes. 'If they want that, let them stay home! Who
needs them? You know what would happen to this
place if you'd put down your fancy hotels? The local
culture would go to hell in a hand basket. Everybody
would be trying to make a buck out of the tourists.
The beach would be crawling with peddlers selling
shells and T-shirts and brass and jewellery and God-
knows-what other junk. Next thing the hookers come,
and from there on it's all downhill.'

'Or uphill, depending on how you look at it,' Adam
countered levelly. He looked at her calmly, hands in
the pockets of his shorts.

'Well, how do *you* look at it?'

'Building and running hotels creates a great number
of jobs, which is good for the local economy, no
question about it.'

'What kind of jobs, though? Chambermaids,
waiters, toilet cleaners, dish washers, doing the dirty
work for the rich foreigners who sit on their behinds
and throw more money around in an hour than they
make in a year! It's obscene!'

Adam frowned in irritation. 'Oh, for God's sake,
Kate, don't sound like a bleeding-heart liberal!
Nobody said life was fair. But what's wrong with
doing honest work for honest wages? And it's damn
well better to make beds and feed your family than
starve in dignified poverty—if there ever was such a
thing!'

She clutched the bag with bananas to her chest. 'It's
a great rationalisation! In the meantime, your
corporation makes fat profits.' It was a stupid
argument, and she knew it. *Her* company was making

profits, too. What had got into her? The heat, maybe
or the smell of the sea or the hot pepper in her lunch.
She pushed her sunglasses back on her nose and
looked at Adam, who was really aggravated now, she
could tell by the hard line of his mouth.

'Kate, for God's sake, don't sound so damned
ignorant! Business generates money that filters down
to *every* level of the economy! You know the
rudiments of economics, don't you?'

Kate gave a deep sigh, and began walking again.
'Oh, I'm sorry. I know you're right. I don't know why
I say stupid things like that. I get carried away because
of my own selfish reasons.' She made a helpless
gesture. 'I like this place the way it is. I'd hate to see it
overrun with tourists with cameras and loud mouths
acting as if they owned the place. The people here are
still real, not trying to imitate everything Western as if
they're ashamed of what they are. They don't try to
hustle you for whatever they can get out of it.' She
shrugged. 'Oh, never mind. We've had this conversation before.'

'All right, let's forget it.'

'On one condition.'

'Yes?'

'Don't go putting down resort hotels on this island!'

Over the next few days they explored the island,
sometimes on foot, sometimes taking trips in the little
coloured vans that transported everything from people
to live goats and dried squid. They ate at the roadside
stands or the tiny restaurants, trying out familiar and
unfamiliar local dishes, drinking Singha beer. They
swam a great deal, made love when the mood struck
them, which was often.

Adam did not talk about making decisions or
mention the fact that he wanted to discuss it. It was a

shadow hovering in the background and Kate was aware of it, like a bruise too painful to touch. Between them was a silent space of unspoken words and thoughts and the knowledge that these few days were only an interlude, a temporary happiness.

The day before they were due to leave, Adam seemed moody, brooding. They'd discussed their schedules, which were, as usual, at odds with each other. It would be two months before they'd both be in New York at the same time again. They'd be too far apart to meet in the interim. She knew what was on his mind and it made her nerves jangle.

'We have to talk,' he said after they'd returned from their lunch. He pulled her down next to him on the side of the bed. 'Kate, I want us to get married. Now. As soon as we're back in the States.'

CHAPTER SEVEN

THE breath stuck in her throat. 'Adam! You can't be serious!' *Married? Now?* She'd expected him to want to talk about finding more time to be together, about her staying in New York more often, but not this. It was so uncharacteristic. He was a man who spent his working days doing feasibility studies, researching, checking into details, making recommendations only with the back-up of endless reports full of figures and graphs. Getting married without even dealing with the problems of their situation seemed like acting against every logical rule. She shook her head. 'It doesn't make sense, Adam. It won't *solve* anything.'

He looked calm and determined. 'We'll *make* sense out of it. We'll work it out. We haven't even begun to look into the possibilities. At least, we'll be married.'

'And what does that mean?' It wouldn't solve a thing. She had no idea what was in his mind. Marriage was no solution. There was no solution for them. There was no choice, no meeting ground.

'Don't sound so defensive, Kate.' He took her hands. 'It will mean a commitment. We'll belong together. We won't be floundering around wondering about our priorities. I want to know that no matter what happens, we're there for each other, that we come first for each other.'

'And we can't do that without marriage?'

He shook his head. 'Not in my book, Kate. Maybe that's old-fashioned, but I just can't see it any other way.'

Her fingernails dug into the palms of her hands. She

felt like she was suffocating. 'Marriage isn't what it
used to be, Adam. Look around you! Divorces galore.
A piece of paper means nothing.'

'It means something to *me* and that's what makes
the difference. And it means something to you, too, or
it wouldn't frighten you so much or make you so
emotional.'

'It doesn't frighten me! I just don't like the idea.
And stop analysing me!'

There was a pause and anger leaped in his eyes.
'You never grew up, did you, Kate? You're still
playing, having fun. God forbid you'd have to stand
still and think out a problem and be a responsible
adult! You want everything, but you simply can't have
it all!'

She jumped off the bed, hands clenched by her side.
'I should never have let you into my life!' she raged, a
potent mixture of anger and pain fermenting inside
her. 'I knew you were trouble the first time I saw you
at Changi Airport!'

'That's irrelevant to the discussion, and un-
productive as well. It's too late now and it can't be
changed. You're wasting your emotions.'

'Don't be so bloody sanctimonious!'

'Meeting each other was inevitable, don't you see
that? You can't fight fate. Fate has its own calendar
and there's nothing you or I can do about it!' The dark
eyes flashed and his mouth was a hard line. He was
angry all right.

Well, she was mad, too. 'I'm not a mindless
creature, victim to all and every whim of fate!' She
took a steadying breath. 'And if we got married I
know damn well what would happen! I'd end up
giving up my career!'

'I didn't ask you to!'

'You have any other solutions?'

'We'll have to work it out. Maybe we could find a way to work together, do something as a team.'

'Well, I don't know how!'

She turned her back to him, looking out of the window, seeing the ocean glittering in the sunlight. Her legs were trembling. She'd never grown up, he'd said. Who did he think he was to say that to her? What was his idea of growing up? What was wrong with having a job you loved, a life that satisfied and gave pleasure? How many people out there were spending their lives in jobs they didn't want and didn't like, dreaming of more excitement, more fulfilment? There was only one life to live and she was going to do it right. She'd worked hard to get the agency off the ground, very, very hard. It was a success story of a kind and she was proud of it. She was using her talents and her capabilities and wasn't that what counted? The sun was beginning to reach into one of the windows, tentative fingers of light slipping through the louvred glass. Kate reached out and jerked the thin curtains shut, leaving the room in a dim golden light.

He was suddenly beside her, grabbing her shoulders to turn her to face him. 'You'd better listen to me,' he said with barely controlled fury. 'Love is not all play and no work! It's not that easy!' His eyes were fixed on her with steely determination. 'You can't go fluttering through life forever! You'll have to make up your mind about what you want out of life and make the investments! If not, you're going to miss out and one day you just may wake up and find yourself alone.'

His sermon infuriated her and she was shaking with it. 'Better happy alone than miserable together!'

Under his tan, his face went white. 'Right,' he said coldly, looking old and hard. 'If that's how you see it, I won't waste your time any more. Goodbye, Kate.' He strode across the room, and she stared at him,

paralysed, as he yanked his suitcase out of the
cupboard and threw in his clothes.

Better happy alone . . . How could she ever have said
such a stupid thing? Kate was in her apartment
stacking plates in the dishwasher, seeing in her mind
Adam's white face when she'd said those words. They
echoed in her mind like an accusation. *Better happy
alone . . . better happy alone . . . better happy alone . . .*

She'd been alone for two months now and she
certainly wasn't happy. In fact, she was miserable. She
hadn't heard from Adam since he'd left Peace Island
after their dreadful argument. No phone calls, no
letters, no funny cards from faraway places. Nothing
but silence.

According to her diary, he had come back to New
York yesterday. Every time the phone rang, her heart
leaped in her chest. It was not realistic to expect him
to call, she knew that. Adam was not the man to come
back once he'd said goodbye. Yet, she kept hoping.
Half-a-dozen times her hand had reached for the
phone, then dropped back to her side. What could she
possibly say to him that would make a difference? *Hi,
this is Kate. Let's get married. I'll give up my career,
have your kids and we'll live happily ever after . . .?*

Her spirits were rock bottom. She was so nervous,
she couldn't eat. She'd dropped a glass and a flower
vase in the space of one afternoon.

'You knew from the beginning it wouldn't work
out,' Roxanne commented. Dressed in black jeans and
a black sweater, she sat at the breakfast bar, munching
sunflower seeds. 'So why are you in such a state?'

'I'm neurotic, obviously,' Kate answered bitterly,
slamming the dishwasher shut. She stared out of the
window, seeing the grey New York buildings soaking
in a drizzle of spring rain. It had rained for days and

days, it seemed, and she'd be glad to get out again next week. Roxanne was leaving tomorrow for a quick trip to Haiti and the Dominican Republic to check up on some villas. She'd be back in a few days. Four days ago Samantha had left for Malawi.

Samantha had a different opinion from Roxanne. Sam was ready to toss everything in for the right man and could not comprehend Kate's dilemma.

'Kate, he's wonderful! One in a million! He's got everything! A good career, intelligence, looks! And he wants to marry you! How can you possibly even *hesitate*?'

Kate had explained. Sam had not understood. 'Aren't you tired of getting on and getting off planes all the time? Think of the freedom you'd have! And right here in New York, for heaven's sake. You'd have time to shop and go to galleries and concerts and plays.' She sighed longingly. 'Find me a catch like Adam and see how fast I'll make up my mind!'

Getting such contradictory advice from her two friends did not help. The agency, the travel was in her blood. It was part of her lifestyle, the way she had grown up—footloose and fancy free. She didn't think she had the capacity to grow roots in a single place.

The next day she said goodbye to Roxanne and spent a long day at the office, her heart making somersaults every time the phone rang. When Becky asked her to come over for dinner, she almost made up an excuse. What if Adam called while she was out? Oh, God, she thought, if I live like this I'll be a mental case in no time. She accepted the invitation and tried futilely all evening not to think of the phone ringing in her empty apartment.

She came home early, having enjoyed the company, but feeling exhausted. She'd been so tired lately, so droopy and without zip. Maybe there was something wrong with her. Maybe she should see a doctor.

The answering machine produced no messages. Deflated, she went to bed. She fell into a deep, dreamless sleep, to be rudely dragged out of it by the ringing of the doorbell. Eyes wide open, she stared into the darkness, heart thudding against her ribs. Good God, who could that be at this hour?

She struggled out of bed, pulled on her robe and rushed to the door. Whimpering sounds came from behind the door. What *was* this?

'Who is it?'

'Adam.'

Her heart made a sickening lurch. She unlocked the door and opened it with shaking hands.

Adam. Looking grey, carrying a crying baby in his arms, and Nicky, looking terrified, clutching his sleeve. It took her a full thirty seconds to take in the scene, staring at them in shocked dismay.

She opened the door wider. 'Come in.'

Adam pushed Nicky in ahead of him, then followed him. Kate closed the door. Adam turned to look at her, holding the baby awkwardly.

'I need your help,' he said.

Without a word she took the baby from him. Its bottom was sopping wet, straight through the blanket wrapped around it.

'What's wrong?' she asked, hugging the baby close, trying to still the crying. She was wide awake now, her mind racing with questions, her heart throbbing painfully at the sight of him.

He ran his hand over the short, curly hair. He looked tired and bewildered and apparently had dressed in a hurry. The colour of his shirt didn't match his slacks and he wore no tie. Her heart cried out for him. Adam! Oh Adam! All the hopeless, helpless love for him rushed to the surface and her body ached with it.

He massaged the back of his neck. 'I had a call an hour ago from one of Sue's neighbours. She'd been taken to the hospital in an ambulance and they didn't know what to do with Nicky and the little girl. They're in their eighties, or nineties, God knows. They didn't know what to do. There was nobody else.'

The crying had changed to howling. Kate looked down on the screwed-up little red face and wondered what to do. Obviously this one needed a dry nappy and probably some food. She didn't know. What she knew about babies was precious little. She had neither nappies, nor a bottle. Could the baby have regular milk? Or would it have to be formula? She hadn't the faintest idea. She didn't even have a book to look it up in. If it wasn't so serious she'd probably laugh at the hilarity of the situation. She took a deep breath. Action was required now, not reflection.

'Here.' She handed the baby back to Adam. 'I'll get a towel and you can put her down on the couch. Then I'll run out and get some nappies. And a bottle, and milk, I guess. There's an all-night supermarket two blocks down.'

He shook his head, frowning. 'I don't want you walking down the street in the middle of the night. I'll go. Tell me what to get.'

She hesitated. She didn't know what to tell him. She'd hoped that looking at the products on the store shelves would give her inspiration. But Adam was probably right. It was ten after two, not the best time to find yourself walking alone in the streets of New York.

'Disposable nappies, formula, a bottle. Just look and make an educated guess.'

'You've got it. Educated guessing is what I do for a

living.' He looked down on the howling infant and
grimaced. 'My God, does she have a voice! Here, take
her!'

Once more she took the baby from him. She
gestured at the keys on the hall table. 'Take these.'

He was out of the door in a flash, obviously relieved
he could do something more useful than stand around
with a wet baby in his arms.

'Sh, sh, sh . . .' Feeling utterly helpless, Kate tried
to calm the baby, cooing and whispering endearments,
all to no avail. She found a towel and spread it out on
the couch and put the baby on it. Suddenly she
became aware of Nicky, sitting ramrod straight on the
edge of a chair, watching her, his eyes dark in the
white face. Her heart went out to him. She'd forgotten
all about him in her worry about his baby sister. She
put a cushion next to the baby so she couldn't roll off
on to the floor and came down on her haunches in
front of Nicky, trying to block out the baby's crying.
It was a nerve-racking sound and it was hard to ignore
the poor mite's distress.

'Hiya, big guy,' she said softly. 'Are you tired?'

He shook his head. 'They took my mommy,' he said
tonelessly. 'In an amberlance.' His eyes filled with
tears. 'The siren was goin' and the lights was flashin'.
I think she's gonna die.'

Her heart contracted. She had no idea at all what
had happened. There hadn't been time to ask. Why
did people get carried off in ambulances in the middle
of the night? Heart attacks, strokes . . . His mother was
too young for those, not even thirty yet. What then?
Acute appendicitis? It could be anything, what did she
know?

'People don't die so easily any more, Nicky. The
doctors are so smart. She'll be fine, you'll see.' Were
those the right words? She had no idea. He stared at

her mutely without giving her a clue as to his thoughts. She wanted to hold him, but he seemed not to want it. He was so contained, so serious. She marvelled at his control.

'How about some milk and cookies? Mr Cooper will be right back with the milk for your sister.' It struck her then that she was responsible for this baby and she didn't even know her name. 'What's her name?' she asked.

'Melissa. But we call her Mellie. I think she's hungry. She cries all the time when she's hungry.'

Kate got up and picked her up again. 'Poor thing,' she whispered. 'Are you so hungry? And we mean people don't give you anything to eat. But we're getting it. Mr Cooper will be back real soon, okay? Why don't you be patient for just a couple of minutes and we'll take care of everything. Dry pants, warm milk. Just a few more minutes.'

The baby was not reasonable. She went on crying lustily, and Kate was beginning to get nervous. What if something else was wrong?

The twenty minutes that Adam was gone seemed an eternity. When she finally heard his knock on the door, relief flooded her.

'Look at this,' he said triumphantly, putting the grocery bag on the coffee table. He fished out ready-to-go bottles of formula. 'Just needs warming up. And here are the nappies. I had to make a guess at the size. Eleven to twenty-three pounds.' He handed her the box.

'Wonderful. Let's get that milk warm, before I have a nervous breakdown.'

A few minutes later the baby was sucking greedily at the bottle, and Kate let out a sigh of relief. She'd changed the nappy while the formula was warming, a task she had never performed in her life. And that at her age. It was a sobering thought. Fortunately, with disposables, it was hardly a challenge, which was just as well. At two-thirty in the morning she was not up to challenges of any sort.

Nicky was drinking milk and munching cookies and Adam was making coffee in the kitchen, the aroma beginning to waft into the room and tantalising her nose. A downright domestic scene, she thought wryly, suddenly struck by the irony of the situation—she and Adam together in an apartment with two small children. It was better not to continue on that train of thought at this hour of the night. She was too tired to think constructively. A yawn escaped her.

She hoped Adam was making Decaf or she wouldn't sleep for the rest of the night—if she ever made it back to bed, that was. She looked down at the baby's face and smiled. Such a soft warm package of contentment now that she was getting what she wanted. Kate felt a rush of sweet, tender feelings. It wasn't a pretty baby. Nothing but a little blonde fuzz for hair, and her ears, like Nicky's, were standing out just a little too much from her head. Yet it was the helplessness that touched her heart. A baby was just a bundle of nerves and instincts, reacting to hunger and cold and discomfort naturally, without thought or reason.

Not like me, she thought. I can't go to Adam, give my emotions free rein and not consider the logical consequences. No. I'm a rational, thinking person, and marrying Adam would not be the rational thing to do, no matter how much I love him or how much I want to be with him.

Adam came back in the room with a tray with two cups and a plate of cookies. 'Decaf for you,' he announced, placing a cup on the table in front of her.

'Thanks. You read my mind. I'll wait till she's finished drinking.' She smiled at him, and he smiled back, his eyes sliding from her face to the baby in her arms.

'She's happy now.'

'Yes. That was easy.'

If only it were easy for us, too, she thought. She glanced over at Nicky, whose eyes were beginning to droop.

'Nicky? How would you like to sleep in the room of a princess?'

His eyes opened wide, then he gave her a disbelieving look. 'A princess? Where?'

She nodded at Samantha's room. 'Over there. Just open the door and have a look.' With all the lace and frills in there he might just believe it. Adam got up and opened the door to the bedroom.

Nicky stared at it for a moment, then turned around and looked at Kate. He made a face. 'It's a girl's room!'

'Princesses are girls.'

He shrugged. 'I guess so. It's pretty fancy though.'

'It is. And the bed is very nice.'

He looked at Adam. 'What about my mommy?'

'Your mom is in good hands. They'll take good care of her in the hospital and we'll see how she is tomorrow, all right?'

Ten minutes later, Nicky was sound asleep in the bed of the princess and the baby lay dozing in Kate's arms, the bottle empty.

'What happened to their mother, Adam?' Kate hadn't dared question Adam with Nicky still around.

Adam shook his head. 'The neighbours didn't know. She was already gone by the time I got to her apartment. Apparently she'd called the emergency number herself and had just managed to give them the address before she passed out. They found her with the phone still in her hand.'

Kate gave a shiver of fear and the baby whimpered in response. 'Oh, God, how awful. And there wasn't anybody to help?'

He shrugged. 'The neighbours on one side are old. Then there's an alcoholic and a nurse working the night shift.' He put his coffee cup down on the table. 'I'd like to go to the hospital and find out what's going on, tell her the kids are okay if they'll let me see her.' He gave her a pleading look. 'Could I leave them with you for the rest of the night?'

'Oh, of course! Sure.'

'Thanks.' He came to his feet slowly, looking down at her holding the sleeping baby against her breast, and the long, yearning look he gave her found an echo in the rush of pain and regret that flooded her.

'Kate . . .?' He closed his eyes briefly, running his hand over his forehead. 'Never mind.' He walked slowly to the door. 'I'll be back in the morning.'

Kate pushed two armchairs together to make a bed for the baby, a trick she remembered from seeing a movie on an aeroplane once. After the baby was settled, she got back into her own bed. Minutes after she'd fallen asleep, Mellie's crying woke her. She pulled the covers over her ears, but the sound was not to be drowned out. With a sigh she got up, took the infant in her arms and walked around the room with her. The sad little sobs shook the tiny body and Kate's heart overflowed with pity. 'Poor girl,' she murmured. 'You miss your own mommy, don't you? I probably don't hold you like she does, and I don't sound like she does.'

After a while the crying subsided and she could feel the baby growing limp against her shoulder. Carefully, Kate lowered her back in her makeshift bed, but immediately the crying began again.

'Okay,' she said, her mind made up, 'we'll do it the way they do it in the rest of the world. Baby sleeps with mama. I'm only a substitute, of course, but that's better than nothing.'

It was a restless night, with the baby bundled close against her, but she managed to get a little sleep. At six the baby awoke and cried. Kate changed her nappy and warmed another bottle of formula, making some strong coffee for herself. She was sitting on the couch feeding the baby when she heard the key in the lock.

Adam came in, carrying a stroller hooked over one arm, and a cardboard box clutched against his chest. It was a strange sight. Adam was a man who carried leather briefcases and expensive suitcases, not torn boxes and baby strollers.

'I was trying to be quiet,' he said. 'I thought you'd still be asleep.'

'Nicky is, but Mellie woke up a little while ago, demanding food. There's a pot of fresh coffee if you want some.'

'Thanks.' He lowered the box to the floor and rested the stroller against a chair. 'I brought some clothes for the kids.'

'How is Sue doing?' It occurred to her then that she had never even met Sue, didn't know what she looked like, what colour hair and eyes she had. And here she was, taking care of two children belonging to a woman she didn't even know.

'Not good. They don't know what's wrong yet. They're doing tests.' He still wore the same clothes, looking utterly weary. She longed to put her arms around him, smooth out the lines of worry on his face. But she could not do that now. Between them was only politeness, the worry over two children and the memories of love.

'Go pour yourself some coffee,' she suggested.

'Yes, thanks, I will.' He was back a moment later, sitting down across from her. She adjusted the baby's weight in her arms, looking at Adam's tired face.

'Have you had any sleep?'

'Sleep? No. I was at the hospital for a couple of hours. They didn't want to talk to me at first. I raised hell.' He smiled wearily. 'They're looking for a next of kin.'

'Did you talk to her?'

'Only for a few minutes. She was very weak, didn't say much, just wondered about the children.' He pressed his hand against the back of his neck. 'She looks awful. She seems wasted, somehow. She was terribly thin, but now ...' He sighed, shaking his head. 'I should have known something was wrong. I should have insisted she see a doctor, but ...' He shrugged. 'She never wanted any interference. She told me she was tired because the baby kept her up at night. I should have known there was more to it than that.'

'Adam,' she said quietly, 'don't be so hard on yourself. Sue is an independent woman, responsible for herself and her two children. Obviously, she wants to make it on her own.'

He tensed at her words. 'Some people can't make it on their own.'

'You can only help when help is wanted.'

He sighed. 'I suppose you're right.'

'She didn't object to your taking the children, did she?'

His mouth curled. 'No. Of course, she had little choice. There wasn't anyone else. No relatives in New York.'

Mellie had finished her bottle. Kate propped her up in the chair-bed and Adam handed her some toys he took from the box.

'When did you get the clothes?' Kate asked.

'I went over there before I came back here. I had the key from last night.' He looked at her. 'Kate, I don't like asking, but could you possibly take the day off? I don't know what to do with the kids on such short notice.'

'I already thought of it. I'll call Becky when the office is open.'

There was warmth in his eyes. 'Thank you. I'll call some agencies today and see if I can get someone to come to my apartment to take care of them.'

'Can I get you some breakfast?'

'I think I'd better go home and get some sleep. I'll go back to the hospital in the afternoon.'

He'd been up all night, running back and forth between his apartment, the children's apartment, her apartment, the supermarket and the hospital.

'I think you've done enough rushing around town for one night. Why don't you stay here? I'll just dress and then you can have my room.' She couldn't put him in Roxanne's. Roxanne was a slob and her bed would be hard to find under all her stuff.

Adam sleeping in her bed. An intimate thought for an unromantic morning. She closed her eyes and turned away. 'I'll fix you some breakfast first.'

He didn't object. He looked too tired to object to anything. He was too preoccupied even to talk while they ate, and afterwards she hastily washed and dressed, straightening the bed quickly before going back to the living-room.

He was playing with Mellie, his face tender, smiling, and the baby was laughing, a delicate, light sound that made her smile. *I want a wife. I want children.* The smile faded from her face as the words came back to her. He would be a wonderful father. He was a loving, caring man who took his responsibilities seriously, maybe too seriously.

'The room is yours,' she said, and her voice sounded strange. She cleared her throat. 'If you tell me where Nicky's school is, I'll take him there.'

He looked up and frowned. 'School? Yes, I suppose so.'

'I think it's better to keep him occupied, don't you think? He'll only worry sitting around here with nothing to do.'

'Yes, of course, you're right.' He gave her the address, stroked Mellie's fuzzy head and disappeared into her bedroom.

Kate had done many things in her life, but she'd never spent a morning like this one. She'd called the office and told them not to expect her in that day. After she'd given Nicky breakfast, she took him to school in a taxi, taking the baby along for the ride. Back in the apartment she picked up the stroller and took Mellie to the supermarket to shop. She'd fed her cereal that morning, on Nicky's instructions, having found a box among the purchases Adam had made in the night. He'd also bought some jars of baby food—vegetables, meat, fruit, and some other items such as baby powder and a pink bib with white ducks on it.

'How am I doing?' she asked Mellie as she put away the few groceries she'd bought. 'Not so bad for an amateur, right?' Mellie gazed up at her from the stroller with big blue eyes, blowing a bubble in answer. Kate grinned. 'Well, thank you. I'm glad you agree. I suppose we should give you a bath sooner or later. I wonder how to go about that. What do you think? Shall we try the sink? Hey, that rhymes! What do you think? Shall we use the sink?' she sang, tickling Mellie's round tummy.

The sink was fine with Mellie. Despite Kate's awkward attempts at washing her squirming little body, Mellie seemed to enjoy her bath. Having accomplished the feat of drying, powdering and dressing the slippery thing, Kate let out a sigh of relief. She hugged the baby close. 'Mmm, you smell real nice. And now how about a nap?' she asked hopefully. It was almost eleven, but Mellie had shown no signs of fatigue. Kate put her down on the two chairs and played with her until the big blue eyes dropped and Mellie drifted into sleep.

Kate sat back in a chair and sighed. She felt exhausted. Well, she hadn't had a very good night and that alone was excuse enough. She grimaced at herself. Taking care of these children was going to wear her out in no time. Riding around on a camel in Inner Mongolia was easier.

She got up and made some fresh coffee. While she waited for the machine to do its thing, she went into Samantha's room and made Nicky's bed.

For a moment she stood in front of her own bedroom door, visualising Adam asleep in her bed. She longed to open the door and look in on him, watch him sleep. She thought of the other mornings when she'd watched him sleep—those blissful lazy mornings when there had been no worries and nothing but time. Long mornings of lovemaking and laughter and leisurely breakfasts in bed.

'Kate?'

Her heart lurched. He had called her. Had he sensed her standing there on the other side of the door? She turned the knob carefully and opened the door a crack. The heavy, lined curtains blocked out most of the light and she couldn't see anything.

'Kate? Is that you?'

'Yes. Did you call me?'

'I did. Come here.'

She advanced into the room, stopping in front of the bed. Her eyes were beginning to adjust and she saw the shape of him in her bed. 'Did you sleep?'

'Yes. What time is it?'

'Not yet eleven-thirty.'

'Nicky in school?'

She nodded, her heart thumping wildly. His chest was bare, the covers pulled up to his waist. He was naked, she knew. He never slept in pyjamas. Naked in her bed. She hadn't seen him for two months—two months since he'd walked out on her on Koh Santisuk.

He reached out and took her head, tugging at it. 'Where's Mellie?'

'Having a nap.' His hand was warm and strong.

He intertwined his fingers with hers. 'Come into bed with me, Kate.'

She shook her head, closing her eyes. 'No, Adam.' Everything inside her yearned for him, but making love would not solve their differences, only make the pain worse.

He leaned sideways, encircled her waist and dragged her on top of him. 'I want you,' he groaned in her ear. 'I want you more than anything. Oh, God, I can't take this any more. Why are you doing this to me, Kate? Why?'

'Please, Adam, no!'

He rolled her over on her back, pinning her against the mattress with his legs and arms. He fumbled with the buttons of her blouse as he kissed her mouth, her throat, her shoulder with hungry impatience. The onslaught shocked her so that she lay still in stunned dismay as he began to strip off her clothes. She'd never seen him this way, so totally out of control. Hot anger washed over her and she began to struggle.

'Adam, stop it! How *dare* you do this to me!'

'Make love to me, Kate,' he groaned, his mouth against her breast. 'Touch me, kiss me.' The naked longing in his voice sparked an answering need in her and desire came rushing back in a wave of feverish warmth. She fought the feelings—she didn't want this she didn't want to be *attacked* like this. Yet sh couldn't fight him, couldn't fight her own bod wanting him, loving him. His skin was hot agains hers, his body hard and wanting and demanding he surrender.

'Adam,' she whispered, 'Adam, this isn't right.' Sh knew she shouldn't allow this. He had no right t force himself on her this way. But he wasn't forcin her any longer, was he? The blood throbbed in he head and she yielded to him in mindless defeat.

It was over quickly. There was no denying sh hadn't wanted him, needed him, still somehow th pleasure had been incomplete. Humiliation was bitte in her mouth.

They lay still for a long time, not speaking, no touching. She didn't know why she didn't move of the bed. She felt numb. It was over and there wa nothing—no warm glow of contentment, no sense o intimacy. Finally Adam propped himself up on on elbow and looked down at her, his eyes filled wit remorse.

'Oh, Kate, I don't know what to say. I don't know what got into me. I'm sorry.'

She felt no anger, no love. 'It's all right.'

'No, it's not.'

'I didn't exactly suffer through it.' She couldn' hide the bitterness in her voice and she saw hin cringe.

'I forced you into it. I had no right. I'm sorry.'

She sat up and swung her legs over the edge of th bed. 'Well, I'm not the first woman that has eve happened to. I'll live.' She picked up her clothes and went into the bathroom, feeling hollow with despair.

CHAPTER EIGHT

It occurred to her, after Adam had left, that finding a housekeeper/nurse in a matter of hours was asking a lot. She looked at Mellie, playing on the chair-bed, and considered the situation. Then, abruptly she picked up the phone and called Becky.

'You'd better count me out for the rest of the week, maybe longer.' In as few words as possible, she explained the situation.

'What about Egypt?' Becky asked. 'Shall I try and get one of the back-ups? Kelly might be able to do it.' The agency used freelance help in emergencies, experienced people who preferred not to work full time but liked to take on a job now and then.

'No. I'm sure Adam will have figured it out by then. Just leave it.'

Figuring things out was not easy.

'I have some interviews set up tomorrow,' said Adam, when he returned later that afternoon. He'd been to the hospital and had picked up Nicky from school afterwards. She'd settled Nicky at the kitchen table with a glass of milk and cookies and told him to do his homework. She followed Adam into the living-room with two cups of coffee.

'I took off from work for the rest of the week,' she said, sitting down across from Adam. 'I'll handle it until Monday.'

He stared at her, then slowly shook his head. 'I can't ask that of you.'

'You didn't.' She bit into a cookie and smiled. 'Now, did you?'

'You have a job to do.'

'The job can wait for a few days. If I'd been sick, couldn't go to work either.'

He was silent for a moment, staring into his cup. 'All right,' he said at last, 'I'll pay you.'

She could feel herself grow cold. '*Pay me?*'

He placed his cup on the table and leaned back in his chair. He'd put on clean clothes, a suit, a shirt and tie, shiny shoes. He looked like the confident business executive working out a deal and she didn't like it.

'I'm taking your time,' he said reasonably. 'I need someone to help me and if you'll do it, I'll pay you. It's a simple business transaction.'

She grew tense with indignation. 'Adam! I don't *want* your money!'

He arched his eyebrows. 'Why not? It's a job.'

She looked straight at him. 'You're offending me.' She got up and turned her back on him, staring blindly at a picture on the wall, trembling with a painful anger.

'Kate, you're being unreasonable. Why would it offend you?'

She turned without answering and walked into the bedroom. She sat on the bed and hugged her knees. He followed her in.

'Don't walk out on me,' he said quietly. 'We're having a discussion.'

'An argument! And I'm not having one with Nick in the kitchen hanging on to our every word.'

He pushed his hands into his pockets and studied her face. 'I want to know why you're offended because I want to pay you for taking care of these children.'

She gripped her knees hard. 'Because it's not what I do. I don't take care of children for money. This is not a simple business transaction! It is an emergency and I am helping out. Don't you understand that? I don't want *payment* for helping.'

'Why would you want to help me?'

'Because you need it! Don't you think I'm capable of just doing something for somebody else?' she asked bitterly. 'Do you think I'm spoiled rotten and selfish and uncaring about other people's problems?'

'I never said that.'

'But you thought it.'

'What in God's name makes you think that?' She could see the angry impatience in his eyes.

'I'm not totally ignorant of my own character flaws, Adam. I've had an easy life. I've mostly lived for my own pleasure. I'm quite aware of that.' She took the pillow and hugged it to herself. 'Well, believe it or not, I just wanted to help you.'

'Kate, I didn't mean to offend you by offering to pay you. It seemed only fair.'

'We're not out in the business world! So stop being the calculating business man! This is a *personal* situation.' She met his eyes. 'But maybe in this personal situation you don't want to feel obligated. Is that it?'

He shook his head slowly. 'I hadn't thought about it that way, Kate.'

'Maybe not, but somewhere in your subconscious it's there. That's why you want to even it out with money.' She swallowed painfully. 'You wouldn't have come to me had it not been for the children, right?'

He closed his eyes briefly. 'Kate . . .'

'Would you, Adam?'

He looked right at her. 'No.'

She'd known it; it wasn't a surprise. Why then did it hurt so much to hear him say it? The pain settled in her stomach and her body tensed, and she saw the reflection of it in his eyes as he held her gaze. *It's no use, no use,* she thought. We're not right for each other.

There was a wail from the living-room. Then another.

Kate sighed. 'It's Mellie.' She got off the bed and Adam moved towards her, putting his hands on her shoulders. Her body grew rigid and she saw him flinch.

'Kate?'

'What?'

'Can we be friends, at least?'

Friends. She didn't want to be his friend, but it was all it could be now. She nodded. 'All right.'

His mouth brushed hers gently. 'Thank you,' he said softly.

She felt her pulse quicken. The pull between them was still as strong as ever, the vibrations that had been there from the moment they'd looked into each other's eyes at the airport in Singapore.

'I'm sorry all this is so painful,' he said quietly. 'I knew you were in town and after I came home myself I went through hell trying not to call you.'

Her throat went dry. 'I know,' she said huskily. 'Me too.'

Their eyes locked for a moment, then she averted her gaze and turned to open the door.

The next two days went by in a blur of exhaustion. The baby cried a lot, obviously missing her mother. Nicky sobbed miserably before falling asleep. Adam came and went, taking Nicky to school, picking him up, taking him to the store to buy new clothes. He helped him with his homework, read him stories and tucked him into bed. Kate found herself watching them, seeing Nicky's adoration of Adam and Adam's patience and affection for Nicky. He played with the baby, making her gurgle with laughter. He gave her the bottle or fed her from a jar. Adam, the devoted daddy. It made her heart ache.

He visited the hospital twice every day and the news was not good. Sue's condition grew steadily worse and the doctors were at a loss. They couldn't find what was wrong with her. A specialist from Yale University Hospital was called in and the tests continued.

The tension between Kate and Adam seemed almost palpable. He was around so much, helping with the children, eating with them, going home only to sleep. Adam's leaving at night was the most painful time of the day, bringing into sharp focus the deterioration of their relationship. It didn't seem right that he didn't stay with her.

Doing the unfamiliar job of caring for a small baby was strain enough and the constant reminder of her own pain was almost unbearable. It hurt to look at him. It hurt to hear him laugh with Nicky. It hurt to be so close to him and yet so far. She yearned to forget it all and hide in his arms.

He didn't kiss her, or touch her. He didn't even smile at her. When their eyes met she averted hers quickly; she couldn't bear to see the pain in his face. Well, she said to herself, it's my own fault, isn't it?

'Kate,' he said Friday afternoon, 'we're going out tonight, you and I. I've got a babysitter lined up for the evening.'

She longed to get out of the apartment, to find some light-hearted fun and laughter, to forget everything if only for a few hours. But she didn't know if it was a good idea to go out with Adam, to spend an evening alone with him. What would they say to each other? Polite conversation with Adam would be more stress, not less.

'I don't know,' she said, hesitating. 'I'm not sure it's a good idea to leave the kids with someone else so soon.' It was an excuse, and a weak one at that.

'We can go after Mellie is asleep. Nicky will be

fine.' He sighed. 'We've got to have some time off, Kate, especially you.'

'I'm all right, Adam.'

'No, you're not, Kate,' he said quietly. 'And I think we need to be with other people. Some friends of mine are having a party. They have a big house in Westchester with an indoor hot tub, so bring a swimsuit.'

She gave a half-smile. 'That's not exactly your thing, is it? Parties, I mean, especially not hot tub parties.'

'Tonight it's just what I need.'

It sounded good, she had to admit. Relaxing in a hot tub with a glass of wine to loosen the tension, some casual conversation ... she could feel herself relax already.

'Where did you get the babysitter?'

'She lives with her parents in my building. She's seventeen and has been babysitting for three years. Don't worry. She's capable and responsible and knows all about babies.'

Kate grimaced. 'That's more than I know at twenty-seven.'

'Don't knock yourself, Kate. You're doing fine.'

She gave a wry smile. 'For me it's nothing short of miraculous. I didn't think I had it in me.'

'We never know until we're put to the test.'

'And I'm getting at least a C minus.'

'An A plus.' He cocked one eyebrow. 'I'm not used to your showing such a lack of self-confidence.'

'You just got a rare look at the real me. Nothing but a bundle of insecurities wrapped up in a lot of pretence.'

He laughed then. 'Hah! Go tell it to some other sucker!'

*   *   *

It was not a large party. There were only two other couples besides their hosts, Bill and Paula.

'Bill and I go way back,' Adam had said in the car. 'We were in college together. He's a Wall Street broker now, doing very well. His wife is a fashion model, very nice.'

Kate found that, apart from being very nice, Paula was also very beautiful with big, lustrous brown eyes, curly black hair and flawless brown skin. She'd grown up in Jamaica, she told Kate, lived in London for three years, then moved to New York. There was an immediate rapport between them and before long they were both laughing helplessly at a story Paula told of her own ignorance when she had first arrived in London at nineteen.

Kate helped Paula carry the trays of snacks to the rec room. Behind a well-stocked bar, Bill, tall, handsome and charming, supplied everyone with drinks. He was talking to Adam as he poured and Adam threw back his head and laughed heartily.

It was good to hear him laugh again. Kate watched him, feeling a flash of insight. *Because he has forgotten about me*, she thought. It shouldn't hurt, but it did. She turned away abruptly.

The house was a beautiful, contemporary-style structure with cathedral ceilings and large glass windows everywhere. It was decorated with flair and personality—Paula's work, no doubt. Kate sat down on an oversized pillow covered in an exotic fabric and took an intersting-looking tidbit from the platter on the low table.

'Would you care for a drink?'

It was Adam, looming large overhead. She swallowed her food and nodded. 'Just some white wine, please.'

He got it for her, then pulled up another one of the

giant pillows and sat across from her, leaning his forearms on his drawn-up knees.

He was being polite, keeping her company. Kate ran her finger round the edge of the glass. 'You don't have to sit with me, Adam,' she said quietly. 'Go talk to your friends. I'm all right.'

'I want to sit here.' He picked up his own glass and took a swallow of his drink. 'How do you like this house?' he asked.

Kate scanned the room. 'I love the spaciousness, those high ceilings, the windows.' She made a face. 'I wouldn't want to have to wash them though.'

'Luckily there are maintenance companies who'll do it for you—at a price, of course.'

'At a price, you can get everything.' She picked up another delectable morsel from the platter and chewed it.

'No, not everything,' he said quietly and her heart jumped. She saw his eyes and the desolation in them made her own pain surface with force.

Love. True love was priceless, not to be had for any amount of money, a treasure not to be bought or sold. So, she said to herself, why am I throwing it away? She looked down in her glass, lifted it to her mouth and drained it.

'Water's hot, folks!'

Kate didn't move. She gazed at the empty glass, wishing there were a way to make the pain go away other than drinking herself into a stupor.

'Are you coming?'

She looked up. Adam was standing over her, reaching out a hand to help her up. She took it, steeling herself not to feel the warmth and the strength of it. He let her go as soon as she was standing.

Kate had brought a one-piece bathing suit. The way

it was cut it didn't cover all that much more than a bikini, yet she felt rather overdressed as she slid into the hot water. The other women, both sleek and tall, had donned only the skimpiest of bikinis.

It was a beautiful room, directly off the rec room. A wooden deck surrounded the large hot tub. Potted palms and hanging baskets with huge ferns transformed the place into an idyllic paradise. Concealed lights threw shadows on the walls and ceilings and flowered cushions lay scattered around the deck. For some reason it made her think of old Rome, of pictures she'd seen depicting the decadent lifestyle of the end of the Roman Empire: rich merchants and patricians lounging around in the baths, food and drink on hand, slaves hurrying in and out at their every command.

No slaves here. Not visible at least. All this stuff needed maintenance, though, and she doubted Paula would go down on her hands and knees and scrub out the tub or clean the deck. No doubt some company or other would take care of that, too.

She looked at Adam sitting in the water across from her. Eyes closed, his head leaning back, he seemed, to the casual observer, totally relaxed. Yet she could see the tension in the lines of his face, in the tightness of the muscles in his neck and shoulders. Why had he taken her with him? she wondered. He should have come here alone; he would have been able to relax more. But that was Adam. He wouldn't go out and have fun, leaving her to cope alone with the children. She needed diversion too, and he knew it.

She surveyed the others. It was rather a cheerful bunch of people, and one of the women had a contagious giggle. Normally she would have enjoyed this, joined in the banter and told jokes and funny stories—she had enough of them to tell. Tonight her mind was too preoccupied. It didn't seem worth the effort to get to know these people, find out their quirks and idiosyncracies, what made them tick. She'd never see them again after tonight.

'You want some more wine?' Bill, next to her, held out a glass he'd picked up from a tray on the wooden deck.

'Thanks.' She took the glass from him and sipped from the cool wine. She smiled at him. 'Very nice.'

'It's French. I'm rather fond of French wines. Adam calls me a snob.'

Kate grimaced. 'Join the club. He calls me a snob, too.'

'Is that so? Well, what does he know? He's just a country boy from upstate New York.'

'Even had a cow,' Kate added.

'Right. Marvellous Minnie.'

Kate grinned. 'And you? Where do you hail from?'

'Me? I've got class. I'm from North Dakota.'

Kate laughed out loud. 'No cows for you?'

He gave her a disdainful look. 'Are you kidding? My father owned the town's dry cleaners.'

Kate laughed again, the sound dying in her throat when she met Adam's eyes across the tub. She took a hasty sip of wine and promptly choked on it.

'Are you all right?'

'I'm ... I'm fine,' she spluttered. 'It's that fancy French wine. It'll do it to me every time.' She took a steadying breath. 'Talking about wine—I was in the south of France last summer. They were selling California wine in the stores and the Europeans were buying it by the case.'

'So I've heard. Adam told me you own a travel agency.'

'I own it with three friends.'

The blue eyes looked at her with interest. 'He said you do a lot of travelling. Do you like it?'

'It's what I do for a living, and I enjoy it, yes. Very much.'

He made a face. 'Not me.' He had brown hair, a bit too long, curling damply around his ears. 'I hate airports, aeroplanes, hotels, strange beds, bad food. I'm always glad when I'm home and can sleep in my own bed again.'

'I didn't think you travelled a lot.'

He grinned. 'I don't. Only a couple of times a year. In the winter we go skiing in Colorado or Austria, and in the summer we go to Greece for my health.' His tone was mildly sardonic and Kate raised her brows.

'For your health?' There seemed nothing wrong with his health, looking at his exterior, anyway. He seemed a rather attractive sample of the male of the species, and there wasn't much hidden from her. He hadn't any superfluous flesh on his bones and he looked strong and muscular, if a bit red and cooked from the hot water.

He grinned. 'We rent a house on a small island for a month. Nothing to do but fish, sail and eat. I like eating, sailing is boring and I hate fishing. I need more action, but Paula is convinced I need to learn to relax or I'll have ulcers or a heart attack.' He rolled his eyes. 'She's teaching me to meditate. Or she thinks she is.' He finished his wine and put the glass down. 'I'm always glad to get back to New York.' He studied her for a moment. 'You think you're going to like living on an island for a few years?' he asked.

She frowned at him in surprise. It seemed a strange question. 'Me? On an island? Where?'

There was a fleeting expression of confusion on his face, then he grinned. 'Oh, I must have misunderstood. You just go places for short times, a few weeks, a month.'

'The longest we've done is six weeks, a camel rid
through the desert in Australia. My friend Roxann
does that one. Maybe that's something for you? N
much fishing out there.'

He groaned. 'I don't think so.' He straightened u
frowning. 'I think I hear the phone.'

'Forget it, Bill!' Paula called out. 'Let it ring!'

With one lithe movement he jumped on to th
deck. 'I can't do that, Pauly. It may be important!'

'It may be important,' mimicked Paula to hi
retreating back. Then she smiled and sighed at th
same time. 'That man is a perfect example c
perpetual motion.' She made a gesture of defeat. '
should just learn to accept it.'

Kate watched Adam slide along the edge of the tu
towards her.

'How do you like Bill?' he asked, relaxing next to her

'I like him. A real workaholic, I bet.'

'The worst. Did he educate you on the stoc
market?'

'Actually, no. We didn't talk about his work. He wa
telling me he hates to go fishing on a Greek island, bu
Paula wants to teach him to meditate to save hin
from ulcers and cardiac arrest.' She grinned. '
suggested a six-week trek on camel-back through th
Australian desert.'

'And he jumped on it.'

'Not quite.'

He was sitting very close to her, naked but for hi
swimming trunks. Bill's body, nice and virile as it was
had not had the slightest effect on her. Adam's was
different story. She knew his body, every inch of it
She knew what happened when she touched him. Sh
knew the feel of it, the scent of it, the taste of it
Leaning her head back, she closed her eyes and bit he
lower lip, hard.

His hand took hers under the water, uncurling her fingers.

'You're not relaxed,' he whispered.

'No.' She yanked her hand away, jumped out of the water and rushed inside into one of the shower cubicles. He followed her in with lightning speed. She leaned against the wall, taking in gulps of air, feeling tears threatening her eyes.

'Did you have to follow me?' she whispered fiercely.

'Yes.'

She glanced at him, then looked away, tears flooding her eyes. She turned, leaning her forehead against the wall, her hands clenched next to her face. He wanted her, too. It would always be this way as long as they were together. She loved him. He loved her. All the conflicts between them didn't make any difference.

She felt his hand on her shoulder, turning her back. He drew her to him and she began to cry.

'I don't want . . . to want you so. I . . .can't . . . take this any longer . . . I can't . . .'

His mouth came down on hers, silencing her. A groan came from his throat and his arms crushed her against his body. Instant fire—smouldering desire bursting into flames. She trembled with it, her blood throbbing in her head. He kissed her eyes, still wet with tears, and his hands moved up and cradled her head.

All the sweet memories surfaced again—of loving and laughing, of the drunken delight they'd found in each other's arms. She ached for him now, aware that this was neither the place nor the time.

Then suddenly he pushed her from him and leaned back against the wall, eyes closed, chest heaving. His hands were clenched by his sides.

She stared at him in shock, her body trembling uncontrollably. 'Adam?'

He opened his eyes and looked at her and despi
the heat of her body she felt herself grow cold. H
face was dark with suppressed rage. Her heart lurche
sickeningly and a shiver ran down her back.

'It was *your* choice, Kate,' he bit out. 'You'll jus
have to learn to live with it! And I'll be damned if
. . . do you know what it's been like for me these pa
few days? Do you have any idea?' he demande
roughly. 'Seeing you with those children, seeing yo
holding that baby . . . do you know what you look lik
when you hold her?' He grabbed her by the shoulde
and there was no tenderness in his touch. His eye
spilled savage anger. 'Why did you have so little trust
After all that time, why didn't you trust me more?'

She stared at him, paralysed by fear as his word
rushed out over her. Her throat was closed and he
tongue wouldn't move.

His face contorted and he thrust her away fror
him. 'Oh, God, what's the . . .'

There was a burst of laughter as the others entere
the dressing area. Adam stopped talking, breathin
hard. The conversation outside the shower stall floate
up over the door.

'You've got to be kidding!' the giggler squealed. 'Ic
cubes? That's cruel!'

Adam took a deep, laboured breath and reached fo
the tap and turned it. They gasped at the same time a
the cold water hit their over-heated bodies. He
muscles tensed and her teeth began to chatter. Sh
thought her heart would give out and fury race
through her. Turning off the shower, she glared a
him.

'You *bastard*!' she whispered fiercely. 'What
rotten thing to do!'

His laugh was short and humourless. 'Well, i
worked, didn't it?'

'It certainly did!'

He opened the door of the cubicle, stepped out and swung it shut behind him, leaving her alone, teeth chattering and tears running down her cheeks.

'Bastard,' she whispered. Her knees gave way and she slid down on to the floor, covering her face with her hands. Everything throbbed with pain—her body, her head, her heart. But worse than that was the memory of his eyes and the violence she'd seen in him.

There was silence for some time, and then the sound of a door opening.

'Kate? Where are you?' It was Paula's softly accented voice and Kate came to her feet and opened the door.

'I'm here,' she said. 'I just took a shower.'

Paula was wearing a pink kimono. She scrutinised Kate's face, then took a towel from a shelf and tossed it to her.

'Here. And don't bother to dress. There's a kimono on the hook over there.' She sat down on a wooden bench that ran along the wall and waited for Kate as she stripped off her swimsuit and dried herself off with the big fluffy towel.

'Trouble in paradise, right?' she said softly.

'You could say that.' Paradise—when was the last time she'd been in paradise? Months ago. She wrapped the kimono around herself and tied the belt with a knot. She began to rub her hair dry, trying desperately to calm herself. She felt bruised inside, her nerves raw.

They went back into the rec room. Everyone was there, all of them sitting around in Japanese kimonos. Adam's back was turned to her as he talked to Bill. Kate studied the others suspiciously. So, what was next?

She sat down on the floor, leaning over towards

Paula. 'Is this where all the men throw their car keys
in the middle?' she whispered. 'Or do we get to see a
blue movie on the video?'

Laughter leaped in Paula's eyes. 'Heck, no. This is
where we all play Trivial Pursuit.'

Later that evening, they drove back home in
suffocating silence and Kate felt sick with misery. The
tension was unbearable, yet there was nothing to say,
nothing to do. She hadn't thought it could get any
worse, but it had. *It was your choice, Kate. You'll just
have to learn to live with it!* She gave him a quick
sideways glance. His face was hard and unyielding as
he stared straight ahead at the dark road in front. He
sat rigidly in his seat as if he was trying to hold on to
his control with every shred of strength he could
muster.

She closed her eyes and leaned her head back
against the seat. It had not been an evening of
relaxation, that much was clear. The air between them
was so charged, she was afraid to breathe. One word,
one sound and something was going to explode.

After all that time, why didn't you trust me more.
What had he meant by that? Trust him that
everything would work out between them, somehow?
Well, she wasn't a romantic teenager with stars in her
eyes.

It seemed an eternity before they were back at her
apartment. They went up in the elevator without a
word, avoiding each other's eyes as if they were
strangers thrown together for only minutes in the
intimate confines of the elevator.

The children were asleep. The babysitter, a
confident, smiling blonde, was watching TV.
Everything was fine, she said. The baby had slept
straight through. She'd read Nicky a book before

putting him to bed. She gave Kate a cheerful good night as she followed Adam out the door.

Adam came back the next morning to take both the children to the park. He did not ask Kate to come along, and she was relieved to find herself alone in the apartment for a couple of hours.

The rest of the day passed with the tension growing rampant. Her stomach felt tight with nerves; she had a blazing headache. She wished Adam would just leave her and the kids alone, or take them away ... something. She couldn't bear having him around. Another reprieve came when he left to go to the hospital to see Sue. But when he came back, she could see by the expression on his face that something was wrong, badly wrong.

'I don't think Sue is going to make it,' Adam said after the children were finally asleep.

Kate stared at him in horror. Her stomach cramped in fear. Suddenly, all her own misery was forgotten. 'Did the doctor say that?'

He nodded. 'They discovered what's wrong with her. That guy from Yale came up with it. Some rare blood disease with a long fancy name. It's a matter of days.' He closed his eyes and rubbed his neck. 'I got a long explanation with all the known details and endless medical jargon.'

'What are they going to do?'

He shrugged. 'Nothing. There's no cure.'

The horror of it filled her with anguish. 'You mean to say they're just going to let her die? Just like that?'

'There's nothing they can do.'

Helpless anger rushed through her. 'She's only twenty-eight years old! She's got two children!'

'I know, Kate,' he said quietly. 'And none of it makes any difference. It's called tragedy.'

'Oh, God . . .' Kate covered her face with her hands. 'I didn't think this would happen, not really. I kept thinking once they knew what it was they could treat it and she'd get better.'

'That's the way we like to think of these things. We want happy endings. We expect them, we feel we have the right to them. But . . .' He shrugged. 'It's just not the way it always goes. Pardon my platitudes.'

Kate stared at her bare toes, the glossy pink nails catching the light. She'd found some time to polish her nails yesterday before going to the party. Such a silly, frivolous thing to do—painting your toenails, going to a party, cooking yourself in a hot tub, playing Trivial Pursuit. And all that time Sue had been lying in bed in the hospital, slowly dying.

She straightened and looked at Adam. 'Does she know?'

He nodded. 'She asked me to take care of the children. She wanted me to be their legal guardian.'

And of course Adam had said yes, she didn't need to ask.

'There's no one else,' he went on. 'Her parents were old when she was born and they're both dead. The only relative she has is a maiden aunt who's crippled with arthritis.'

'What about her in-laws?'

He shook his head. 'Nobody. Her husband grew up in foster homes.'

Kate stared at him in numb disbelief. 'I can't believe this,' she whispered. She thought of her own relatives—parents, a brother, a sister, aunts, uncles, cousins—an endless number of them. She couldn't conceive of being so alone in the world, of having no one at all to turn to. It made her ache with pity. 'So, now what?' she asked.

'She said to have them adopted, but she wanted

me to take care of it and make sure they'll stay together.'

There was a knot of sadness in her stomach. She wondered about the terrible despair Sue must be feeling, planning for her children's future. She had never felt more compassion for anyone in her life.

They sat in silence until finally Adam came wearily to his feet. 'Well, I'd better go home. How about if I come by in the morning and we take the kids to the zoo?'

The zoo. Something else so frivolous. Yet it was important, too. Important to bring some joy into Nicky's life.

'Fine. They'll enjoy it. Nicky at least.'

But they didn't make it to the zoo. Soon after he got up Sunday morning, Adam received a phone call from the hospital telling him that Sue had died.

CHAPTER NINE

'WHAT'S going to happen? What will you do?' Concerned, Kate looked at Adam. His face looked drawn, his eyes dull. It had been a terrible day with Nicky crying hysterically until he'd collapsed from exhaustion. He was sleeping now in Samantha's bed, hugging a teddy bear.

'Someone from Social Services is coming to talk to me tomorrow.' He straightened in his chair, looking directly at her. 'I'm not going to give them up for adoption,' he stated.

Kate stared at him. 'You're not? What are you going to do, then?'

'I want to keep them. I'll adopt them myself.'

Her throat went dry and she was bereft of speech. 'You can't be serious,' she whispered at last. 'Adam, you can't do that!'

'Why not?'

Kate got up out of her chair and stood in front of him. 'You're never home! How are you going to take care of a baby and a little boy?'

'I'll do something about my schedule,' he said calmly. 'And I've found a woman who'll live in. She's very good.'

Kate shook her head in bewilderment. 'You're not realistic, Adam. Children need parents, not a father who's never home and a paid housekeeper!'

He came slowly to his feet, his jaw hard, his eyes angry.

'I'll deal with it!'

'But it isn't in the best interests of the children

don't you see that? They'd be better off with an adoptive family, or a foster family.'

His eyes were cold. 'What makes you the expert?'

'It's just common sense!' She was almost shouting at him. She couldn't believe this was happening. 'Besides, it won't be your decision, have you considered that? You may be their guardian, but the court still has to rule whether it's in their best interests to stay with you or go to an adoptive family.'

His eyes narrowed. 'I'm well aware of that.'

'Adam, you're not rational.'

'You don't need to insult me,' he said coldly.

'It's not meant as an insult! I just don't understand you!'

No, it wasn't rational. Yet Adam was not an irrational person. So why was he doing this? Why was he taking on this responsibility? She stared fixedly at his angry face, and a flash of insight brought the answer. It was suddenly clear to her and it made her angry, angrier than she'd ever been at him.

She fought for control. 'Those children are not your personal responsibility, Adam,' she said in a low voice.

'I'm making them my responsibility!'

'There's got to be a limit, Adam! There's got to be a limit to those unreasonable, irrational *guilt* feelings of yours! It's *not* your fault their mother died. It's *not* your fault that their father was speeding and skidded on the ice in front of your car! You're *not* responsible!' She was trembling with anger. She anchored her feet to the floor, steadying herself.

His mouth twisted. 'Quite the psychoanalyst, aren't we? Did you really think that I'm motivated by guilt?'

'Yes! That's why you started taking Nicky out to start with. You've *told* me how guilty you felt! You feel guilty because you couldn't do more for Sue,

widowed, pregnant, poor, and too damned proud to let
you help.'

'You're wrong,' he said with icy anger. 'I want those
children and it has nothing to do with guilt! I want
them for pure selfish reasons! I don't want Nicky to go
anywhere else. I don't want anybody else to be his
father.' He paused. 'I love that boy. I want him for my
son.' He looked right at her. 'And I'm going to do
whatever it takes to convince the Department of Social
Services to give both those children to me.'

She felt defeated and stared at him without
speaking. There was no way she was going to make
him see his folly. Their eyes locked and a shiver went
down her spine. He was like a stranger, his eyes
devoid of warmth as he looked at her.

'Kate,' he said, his voice low, 'what's it to you?'

It was like a slap in the face. She felt the colour
drain from her cheeks. Without a word she turned and
walked into the bedroom, locking the door behind her.

What's it to you? What's it to you? She buried her
face in the pillow. 'Nothing,' she muttered. 'It has
nothing to do with me.'

After all, she'd had the offer, hadn't she? He wanted a
wife and children, and he'd asked her. And she'd said no.
So what was it to her if he wanted these two children?

It's nothing to me, she thought. It's none of my
business. You do what you have to do, Adam Cooper.

Wednesday morning. Kate was folding baby clothes
and putting them in a box with tired, mechanical
movements. Nicky was back in school, Mellie was
having her nap and Adam was taking the housekeeper
to his apartment, two days later than had been
anticipated. If Adam was allowed to keep the children,
he would look for a bigger place and Mrs O'Brian
would come and live in.

How they had made it through the past few days, Kate didn't know. Nicky had withdrawn and stared mutely off into space for hours on end. Nobody could reach him, not Kate, not Roxanne who had returned from the Dominican Republic Sunday afternoon, not even Adam.

Adam. Her heart ached at the thought of him. They were nothing more than polite strangers. She lay awake at night thinking about him, about the children. Would the court let him adopt them? It didn't seem likely. They needed a normal family setting and Adam could not provide that. If they took the children from him, how would he react? He loved Nicky. He didn't know Mellie as well, but he played with her and made her laugh, showing a gentleness and tenderness that made Kate grow warm and soft inside.

She had finished with the baby clothes. Nicky's were already done. Later this afternoon Adam would come for the children and take them home with him. The apartment would return to its former quiet order. Roxanne had not complained, but had pitched in and helped, done the shopping, taken the baby out for a walk in the park in the squeaky stroller.

'I met an old flame of mine,' she commented with a chuckle when she came back. 'Thought I'd settled down to marriage and motherhood. Can you imagine? Not me, I told him, not for love or money.' She took Mellie out of the stroller, hugged her and tickled her until she hiccupped with laughter. 'I'll make a super aunt one day, at least if my little brother will hurry up and make me one.' She nuzzled the baby's neck. 'Aunty Roxanne—how does that sound?'

'Mommy sounds better,' Kate said drily, watching her. 'To her at least.'

The smile faded from Roxanne's face. 'Yes, sorry. I wasn't thinking.' She handed Mellie back to Kate.

'Poor mite. She'll have one though. Couples who want to adopt babies are lined up from here to to San Francisco.'

'Adam wants them both.'

Roxanne's eyes widened and her mouth fell open. 'You're kidding me.'

Kate shook her head. 'No.'

'That's crazy!'

'That's what I said.'

'How is he going to take care of them? He's *gone* all the time?'

'I asked him that, too.'

'And what did he say?'

'He'll work it out. Don't ask me how. He'll get a housekeeper, do something about his work schedule. Maybe he'll forget about his career in the hotel business and do something else.'

'Not Adam.'

Kate gave a small smile. 'Adam may surprise you one of these days. Your image of Adam is rather flawed, you know, Roxanne. I think you've never forgiven him for beating you at chess.'

Roxanne waved her hand in dismissal. 'Who says he'll actually get to keep those kids? Doesn't a judge have to decide that or something?'

'Yes, but Sue did appoint him as their legal guardian before she died.'

Roxanne shrugged. 'Being a guardian doesn't mean you're a fit parent.'

'I know.'

What if the court won't let him keep them? The question had haunted her for the past three days and nights. It was the reason she couldn't sleep, the reason she couldn't seem to get food past her throat. She stared blindly at the baby clothes in the box.

'Don't even *think* of it,' Roxanne had said the night

before.

'Think of what?'

'Marrying Adam. And you know that's what I meant.'

Kate gave no reply. The apartment was silent. The children were asleep and Adam had gone home.

'If you marry him, the court might give him those children, that's what you're thinking, right?'

'Yes.'

'Don't do it, Kate. You'll be miserable.'

Kate looked at her defiantly. 'Why?'

'You know why! Marrying Adam is one thing—wrong too—but, marrying *Adam plus two children* is madness! You'll have to give up your career, play mama to a little baby and sit at home all day. It's not you, Kate. You'll go crazy!'

Roxanne was right, she knew, yet it angered her to hear her be so blunt about it, so cold and calculating, as if love and feelings weren't involved.

Kate picked up the box and put it near the door. If it were only a matter of reason, of logic, it would be so simple, she thought. What Adam had decided to do was his problem, not hers. She had nothing to do with it. She was responsible for her own happiness only. She didn't owe him or the children or Sue anything.

But she loved Adam, and that made all the difference in the world.

There has to be a way, Kate thought. *There has to be a solution.*

Maybe she could take a trip once or twice a year while Adam stayed at home. He should be able to take some leave of absence now and then, or maybe he could apply for a job in the company that didn't involve quite so much travel. Maybe that's what he was planning to do already, anyway. And the baby wouldn't be tiny forever. In a few years everything would look easier.

A few years. She closed her eyes, feeling panic rise again. *What if I'm not happy staying home? What if I can't take being tied down by two kids?* She went into the bedroom and looked at the sleeping Mellie and her heart melted. She needed a mother, not a stand-in, hired housekeeper. And Nicky, who'd gone through so much, who had lost both his father and mother before he was even seven—he needed loving and nurturing to chase away the sadness in his eyes.

And there was Adam.

Adam, who didn't smile anymore except when he spoke to the children. The light had faded from his eyes, his vitality had vanished. *He needs me too.*

And I can't live without him, she thought. I can't give him up. She thought of the weary look on his face, the tired lines around his mouth. He can buy a housekeeper, babysitters, nannies. But he can't buy love and he needs it—we all need it, all four of us.

He came for the children later that afternoon. Everything was arranged. Mrs O'Brian, the housekeeper, was waiting for them at Adam's apartment.

Kate carried the children's meagre possessions to the car, following Adam, who carried the baby. He gently put her down in a babyseat in the back and strapped her in. He'd even thought of that, a babyseat. Kate felt her throat close up. Adam motioned Nicky to sit in the back too and told him to put on his seat belt.

Kate leaned into the car, kissing them both for the last time, her throat aching with the effort not to cry.

'I'll bring you something from Egypt,' she said to Nicky, her voice squeaky. Oh, God, she thought, listen to me! *I'll bring you ... I'll give you ... Anything, anything, but I can't be with you, because I'd rather be out there playing the field.*

His skinny arms clung to her neck. 'You'd better let

go, Nicky,' she said softly. 'It's time to go.' *You'd better let go ... you'd better let go ...*

'I want you to come with us,' said Nicky, looking scared.

She steeled herself against her emotions. 'I can't. I have a job, Nicky. Fourteen people are waiting for me in Egypt.' *Fourteen spoiled, rich people who need me to show them a good time. Fourteen people who want their money's worth.* 'I'll come and see you when I get back, okay?'

His arms dropped away from her neck. 'Okay,' he said tonelessly.

She stroked Mellie's fuzzy head once more and straightened away from the car.

Adam was looking at her, eyes unreadable. 'I don't know how to thank you for what you've done,' he said quietly. 'You were the only one I could think of to turn to. I won't forget, Kate.'

'It's all right, Adam. I wanted ... to help.' She could barely get the words out, and she was terrified of bursting into tears right there in the parking lot. She took a step back. 'I hope everything will be all right. I'll call when I get back from Egypt.'

He nodded. 'Have a good trip. Goodbye, Kate.'

'Goodbye, Adam.'

He slid behind the wheel and started the engine. No kiss, no hug. Not even a handshake. Strangers were all they were. Kate rushed inside, not looking back. She ran up five flights of stairs, tears running down her cheeks, until she couldn't move her legs any more and sank down on the cold steps, breathless and shivering with her sobs.

If she didn't do something now, it would be too late. She'd lose Adam forever.

She came to her feet slowly, taking the last flight of stairs in dazed numbness. In her apartment all was quiet. She glanced around and shivered. Silent, empty, dead.

Peace, she thought. It's what I wanted. Peace and quiet and my precious freedom. Then her eyes caught the book on the couch. Nicky's book, with its bright red and blue cover, the one Adam had bought for him. An image flashed into her mind—Adam on the couch, with Mellie in his right arm and Nicky hugging his left as he read him the book. And there was nothing else in her mind but the picture of the three of them huddled together on the couch. She clenched her hands and closed her eyes and it was still there; it would forever be there.

She sank down on the couch and pressed her hands to her face. 'Oh, Adam,' she moaned, 'I can't let you go.' She took a deep, shuddering breath, feeling tension flow from her body. 'I'm not going to let you go,' she whispered.

She went to him the next evening, taking a taxi to his apartment. She hadn't had the courage to call him to tell him she was coming.

He opened the door himself and she saw the surprise flare in his eyes when he saw her.

'Hello, Kate.'

'Hi. Can I talk to you?'

'Of course, come in.' He led her into the living-room. 'Can I get you a drink? A cup of coffee?' So polite, so formal. Her stomach churned. He sat down opposite her in a chair. She looked around the room, unsure about how to start. The room looked different, the furniture rearranged to accommodate a playpen, a yellow affair with bunnies hopping over the pad on the bottom. Nicky's toys lay in disarray in one corner of the room.

'Are they asleep?' she asked.

He nodded.

'My place is so empty without them,' she said nervously.

He gave a half-smile. 'And mine is so full.'

'Yes.' She got up, jamming her hands into her jeans. 'I'll have that drink after all, if you don't mind.'

Minutes later she held the glass of wine in her hands. 'I don't know where to begin,' she said miserably.

'How about the beginning?'

She closed her eyes briefly. 'Adam, I ... I love you.'

There was a moment of quivering silence. 'I love you too, Kate.'

Oh, please, she prayed, don't let me cry now. She looked at him through a haze of tears. 'In Thailand you asked me to marry you.'

'I did.'

'Do you still want me?'

'I'll always want you, Kate.'

She swallowed at the constriction in her throat. Her hands trembled and she put the wine glass on the table. 'Can we please get married, Adam?'

He stood very still, his face inscrutable. Then he slowly shook his head. 'I don't know that it's such a good idea any more, if it ever was to begin with.'

She could feel the tears press behind her eyes. 'Adam, I don't want to go on without you. I'm sorry about that fight we had, about the things I said. But I was selfish and immature and, and ... scared.' Her voice shook.

'Scared of what?'

'Of committing myself, of giving up my career, of a hundred things.'

'And now?'

She wiped her hand across her eyes. 'I'm even more

scared, but Adam, I . . .' Her voice trailed away and she made a helpless gesture with her hand.

He was still standing where he had been ten minutes before, hands in his pockets. 'There are the children, Kate,' he said quietly.

'That's why I came.' She ran her tongue over her dry lips. 'I can't let you deal with this alone, Adam. Maybe . . . as a couple there's more chance we'll get them.'

There was a silence and he scanned her face with dismay. 'Why, Kate?' he asked at last. 'Why would you want to do that?'

'Because I love you! Because I know how much want them, how much you care!' She swallowe didn't want to find out later that the children gone and I had done nothing to help you.'

'I thought you didn't want me to have them,' in said slowly. 'You said they'd be better off with an adoptive family. If I don't get them, that's where they'll probably go.'

'But you won't be happy! If we get married we'll be a family. They'll have what they need, a father and a mother.' She sat down in a chair and hugged herself.

He turned to the window and stared outside. 'So,' he said slowly, 'the children will have parents. I'll have the children, and a wife.' He turned to face her. 'What's in it for you, Kate?'

'I'll have you. You, and the kids.'

His eyes bored into hers. 'And is that enough?'

Her palms were clammy and she wiped them off on her jeans. 'Love is more important than any job, Adam.' And then the tears came, blinding her. 'I don't want to lose you. I love you. I love you so much that nothing else seems to matter. Maybe it's stupid to say that, but it's true. All that matters is you, and whatever happens, I'll deal with it.' She squared her shoulders and smiled through her tears. 'I'm tough, you know. I've made so many new beginnings in my life—new countries, new schools, new friends. I always adapted. I'll adapt again, somehow.' She took a shuddering breath. 'It's time I grew up. I just hadn't expected to do it quite so instantly.'

A smile briefly tugged at the corners of his mouth, then disappeared and his eyes were dark and brooding again.

'Oh, Adam, don't look at me like that!' She jumped up and came to where he was standing, stopping inches away. 'Please, Adam,' she said huskily, 'tell me you still want me.'

She saw something in his face, something breaking as he hauled her to him, holding her so tight she gasped. 'I'll always want you, Kate. I'll always love you,' he said hoarsely. 'I can't believe you're here. Are you sure? Are you really sure?'

She nodded. 'I've made up my mind. I've already quit my job. I'm not going to Egypt tomorrow.'

He grew still against her. 'You're not?'

'No.'

He drew back a little, looking into her eyes. 'You're absolutely sure?'

'Yes. Petrified, but sure.' She fought the black wave of fear that threatened her mind—no more flying free, no more trekking through deserts or lazing on palm-shaded beaches. No longer the sights and sounds and smells of places foreign. Images passed before her eyes—women in jewel-coloured saris, bullock carts stacked high with produce, the sun setting on a tropical beach ... Sounds played through her mind—the rhythm of African drums, the thrill of a Kashmiri flute, the monotonous kling-klang of a Javanese gamelan band, the silence of the desert ... She took a deep breath. From now on, every day she would wake up in the same bed, sit at the same breakfast table, see the same faces. But they were the faces she loved, more precious than all the faces that had passed through her life until now.

Adam reached out and brushed a curl from her forehead, smiling at her ruefully. 'Kate, I never asked you to give up your career, you know. You *assumed* I'd want you to.'

'There isn't much choice now, is there?'

'There are always choices, Kate. What hurt me most when we had that argument was that you were so sure I'd ask you to give up your work. I'd hoped we could have figured out something together, make some compromises. But you were so full of defences and negative assumptions that I couldn't take it. It seemed you didn't even want to *think* of working it out.'

'I'm sorry,' she said softly. 'It was just the way it always was, Adam. Please understand. Nobody ever took my work very seriously. I was always expected to make the sacrifices. I just assumed you were like the others.' She grimaced. 'Listen to me. It sounds like I had an army of lovers. I didn't mean it that way.'

He looked into her eyes. 'I don't know where you got the idea that I was such a male chauvinist. I felt demeaned. I thought you knew me better than that, yet you threw me on a heap with the rest of them, effectively calling me selfish and inconsiderate of your needs and feelings. I didn't deserve that.'

She'd never felt so small in her life, felt herself shrinking under his words. She didn't dare look at him.

He lifted her face, forcing her to meet his eyes. 'Why didn't you trust me more, Kate?'

She shook her head. Her throat felt dry. 'I don't know. I'm an imperfect flawed human being, not to speak of stupid and blind.' She swallowed. 'We never talked about it.'

'The subject was taboo, Kate. As soon as I made the mildest comment, you'd withdraw. That first night in New York you wouldn't even have dinner with me until I promised not to mention living together, marriage, careers for six months.'

It was true. She had no defence, no excuse. 'I'm sorry, Adam. Please forgive me.' It sounded a little dramatic and it made them both smile. 'I mean it,' she added, resting her face against his chest. 'I've been so miserable ever since you left me.'

'So have I.' He ran his fingers through her hair. 'Kate,' he said quietly, 'your happiness is very important to me. It always was. I never had any intention of making a grass-widow-housewife out of you if you didn't want that. I've tried to look for alternatives, some lifestyle that would suit us both.'

'Now we have two children. It'll be a challenge.'

He released her, stepping back. 'Let's sit down.' He pulled her down next to him on the sofa. 'I talked to a number of people—colleagues, friends, others in the hotel and tourist business, to see what could come out of it. I put out feelers, kept my eyes open.'

'And?'

'How would you like to live in Indonesia for a few years?'

'Indonesia? What do you mean?'

'Somebody called me about a project, a different sort of resort, on Kalimantan, inland on the Mahakam River. No sprawling multi-storey building with tennis courts and swimming pool and the rest. It'll be set up like a Dayak village with traditional longhouses and it will be integrated as much as possible with the local way of life, with some necessary exceptions, of course.'

Incredulous, Kate gaped at him. 'Adam! That was *my* idea! That's the sort of thing I've been talking about!'

He gave a crooked grin. 'I know. And I shot i
down.'

'You said there's no money in that kind of thing.'

He shrugged lightly. 'I'm still not sure about that.
The idea is to duplicate these villages the world over.
each one different because it will be adapted to its own
locality. A whole new concept in vacationing.'

'But ... you said nobody would finance a venture
like that because it's not a profitable proposition.'

'Nobody but an eccentric old man with more money
than he knows what to do with.'

An eccentric old man ... A memory stirred.
'McCoy?' she asked in amazement. McCoy, the multi-
millionaire who owned the villa on the Riviera, the old
man who'd spent twenty years in Borneo, which was
now the Indonesian island of Kalimantan, apart from
the northern section, which belonged to Malaysia.

'The one and only.'

Kate gave a wide grin. 'Oh, I knew he was my kind
of guy! But what made him decide to do this?'
Excitement, like fever, crept through her. She stirred
restlessly. 'Tell me about it, Adam!'

'He has some very special feelings about Borneo—
Kalimantan, and you're the one who gave him the
idea. You must have convinced him.'

She nodded slowly. 'I talked to him about that, I
remember now.' That last evening in France, they'd
sat on the terrace of the villa and talked. She'd told
him of her job and her ideas and he'd been very
interested. He'd told her of his canoe trip down the
Amazon, which had seemed a rather hair-raising
expedition, even to Kate. The man was, after all, not
exactly in the prime of life.

'When did he tell you about this?' she asked.

'Last week.'

'You didn't tell me,' she said, her voice low.

'No.' He paused. 'He wanted both of us, and I told him we were no longer together and I was not interested.'

She searched his face. 'Why didn't you tell me?'

His eyes held hers and for a moment there was silence. Then he released her and pushed himself to his feet. He raked his hand through his hair, looking down at her.

'Kate . . .' he began with obvious difficulty, 'when I left you in Thailand I had decided not to see you again. It was over. You believed the worst of me. You had no faith in me, or in us. I couldn't forgive you for that.' He paused. 'When this McCoy project came through, I wondered of course if it would make a difference. But I had my pride. I didn't want you to want me because we could both have a job on some exotic tropical island. I wanted you to want me because you *loved* me, because you wanted to share your life with me no matter what. I wanted you to be willing to work things out together. And it didn't seem to be that way. It seemed that to you your career came first. And that I couldn't take, Kate.'

Kate felt a deep shame, seeing herself for the very first time the way he must have. She'd been self-centred and self-serving. And she'd had no faith, no faith in him or in their love.

'And now?' she whispered.

'Oh, Kate!' He sat down again, gathering her against him. 'You gave up your career for me, and for two children to whom you owe nothing.'

'I love you,' she said huskily. 'I couldn't just let you go through all this alone.'

His arms tightened around her. 'I know.' His mouth found hers. 'I love you, too,' he muttered against her lips. 'I love you, too . . .' It was a long, lingering kiss, full of love and tenderness and sweet delight. Then he drew away, looking into her eyes with dark intensity.

'Will you marry me, Kate?'

Joy leaped through her. 'Yes, I will.'

'No matter what?'

'No matter what.'

He expelled a long sigh, drawing her close again. 'We'll be happy on Kalimantan, Kate. We'll work together to make this resort a success. With George's money, your creativity and my business sense, how can we lose? Your agency can get us the clients. We'll have our own place and someone to do the housework, and a girl to help with the children so you won't need to be around every minute of the day. But we'll both be home and we won't be travelling.'

'But you said you told McCoy you weren't interested.'

'George told me he'd give me a month to change my mind. And then made me an offer that was very, very tempting, with the provision that you be included in the deal.'

'What about school for Nicky?'

'There will be other American children. There's a team of people involved in this venture – an anthropologist, an engineer, an architect, a sociologist, people like that. We'll bring over a teacher. And there'll be plenty of Indonesian children to play with.'

'It sounds like it's all organised already.'

'McCoy's been working on the proposal and the plans ever since last summer.'

'Adam,' she said after a moment of thought, 'you'll have to resign from the Crown Hotel Corporation. What about your career?'

He shrugged. 'I'll have another one. It's still in the same general business. Careers aren't everything, Kate. I found that out.'

She shook her head slowly. 'That doesn't sound like

you at all, Adam. Doing something so ... so spontaneously.'

He smiled ruefully. 'I've probably been a little too rigid before. What we're going to do now may be a bit risky, but it'll be fun trying.'

'Yes, but Adam ... is this really what you want?'

He took her face in his hands and looked deep into her eyes. 'What I really want, Kate, is right here in this apartment—love, a wife, kids.' He kissed her then and all the worry and fear flowed out of her. There was only warmth and a deep, overwhelming love that filled her with peace.

A noise distracted them. They drew apart, seeing Nicky standing in the door, rubbing his eyes.

'I was dreaming my mommy came back,' he said on a low note. He advanced into the room. 'But it can't happen, can it?'

Her heart ached at the sadness in his face. 'No, it can't happen, Nicky. Come here, sit with us.' She moved over to make space between her and Adam. He sat down, leaning his head against her.

'Your mom can't come back in person, but she can be with you in your thoughts and in your heart,' she said quietly.

'Before I go to sleep, I talk to her.'

'That's good, Nicky, she likes that.'

'You think she can hear me in heaven?'

'Yes, I'm sure she can.'

'Why are you here?' he asked as if he had only now realised she wasn't supposed to be there. 'I thought you was goin' away. Or is this a dream, too?'

Adam grinned, drawing him close to him. 'No, it's not a dream. Kate decided she'd rather be with us than go to Egypt with a bunch of strangers.'

He sighed. 'I'm glad. You're nice, Kate. Will you bake me some molasses cookies tomorrow?'

'I sure will.'

'And now, young man,' said Adam, 'it's time to get back to bed. Come, I'll tuck you in.'

'I want Kate to come, too.'

'Okay, I'll come, too.'

Later, Kate lay in Adam's arms in the big bed, basking in the afterglow of lovemaking. It had never been better, more passionate, more loving, more satisfying. *Because now we really belong to each other*, she thought, giving a deep contented sigh.

'Adam,' she said softly, 'I've been so stupid, so blind. I don't know why I ever thought you were just like the others when you asked me to marry you.' Absently, she trailed a finger through the curly hair on his chest. 'You're not, you know. The same, I mean.'

'I'm sure not,' he said drily. 'I'm just a dull, conservative guy who wears ties to parties.'

'You are the most exciting man I know. And you can wear a tie to bed, for all I care.'

'Kate!' he said, feigning shock. 'I said *dull*, not *kinky*!'

She snapped her fingers, grinning wide. 'Oh, heck!'

Harlequin Presents

Coming Next Month

983 STANDING ON THE OUTSIDE Lindsay Armstrong
An Australian secretary is drawn out when her new boss goes out of his way to make her smile…enjoy life again. But what's the point if his heart still belongs to his childhood sweetheart?

984 DON'T ASK ME NOW Emma Darcy
How can a country girl from Armidale trust her heart to her uppercrust business partner? Especially when his attraction coincides with the renewed interest of the first man to reject her as not being good enough to marry.

985 ALL MY TOMORROWS Rosemary Hammond
In war-torn San Cristobal a nurse falls hard for an injured reporter, who then disappears from her life. She knows she must forget him. But how can she, when he finds her again in her home town?

986 FASCINATION Patricia Lake
Emotionally scarred by the last suitor shoved her way, a young American finds a merchant banker difficult to trust—particularly when their bedside wedding in her grandfather's hospital room is arranged by her grandfather and the groom!

987 LOVE IN THE DARK Charlotte Lamb
The barrister an Englishwoman once loved threatens to revive the scandal that drove them apart five years ago—unless she breaks off with her fiancé and marries him instead.

988 A GAME OF DECEIT Sandra Marton
A magazine reporter, traveling incognito, wangles an invitation to stay at a famous actor's private hideaway in the Mexican Sierra Madre. But she's the one who begins to feel vulnerable, afraid of being exposed.

989 VELVET PROMISE Carole Mortimer
A young divorcée returns to Jersey and falls in love with her ex-husband's cousin. But he still thinks she married for money. If only she could tell him how horribly wrong he is!

990 BITTERSWEET MARRIAGE Jeneth Murrey
Turndowns confuse a job-hunting woman until she discovers the souce of her bad luck—the powerful English businessman she once walked out on. Finally he's in a position to marry her!

Available in June wherever paperback books are sold, or through Harlequin Reader Service:

In the U.S.	In Canada
901 Fuhrmann Blvd.	P.O. Box 603
P.O. Box 1397	Fort Erie, Ontario
Buffalo, N.Y. 14240-1397	L2A 5X3

Take 4 books
& a surprise gift
FREE

SPECIAL LIMITED-TIME OFFER

Mail to   **Harlequin Reader Service®**

In the U.S.   In Canada
901 Fuhrmann Blvd.   P.O. Box 609
P.O. Box 1394   Fort Erie, Ontario
Buffalo, N.Y. 14240-1394   L2A 5X3

YES! Please send me 4 free Harlequin Romance® novels
and my free surprise gift. Then send me 6 brand-new novels every
month as they come off the presses. Bill me at the low price of
$1.66 each*—a 15% saving off the retail price. There are no
shipping, handling or other hidden costs. There is no minimum
number of books I must purchase. I can always return a shipment
and cancel at any time. Even if I never buy another book from
Harlequin, the 4 free novels and the surprise gift are mine to keep
forever.   116 BPR BP7S

*$1.75 in Canada plus 69¢ postage and handling per shipment.

Name _____ (PLEASE PRINT) _____

Address _____ Apt. No. _____

City _____ State/Prov. _____ Zip/Postal Code _____

This offer is limited to one order per household and not valid to present
subscribers. Price is subject to change.   DOR-SUB-1A

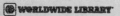